"I didn't hire you on a temporary basis."

He continued with irritating assurance. "Unlike Howard, I have no plan to return to America. So who can tell—if you play your cards right you could still be with me in years to come."

Thrilling prospect, Kate thought. He had to be kidding. The grin tugging at the corners of his mouth suggested that he was.

"In that case, perhaps you could give me some work to get on with," she replied, her own smile blatantly false, "so I can impress you."

"Oh, but you have already." Van's appraisal was slow and thorough and far too personal. "Beautiful as well as smart. What more could a man ask for...in a secretary?"

"Inexhaustible patience!" Kate snapped as hers finally ran out.

Books by Alison Fraser

These books may be available at your local bookseller.

Don't miss any of our special offers. Write to us at the following address for information on our newest releases.

Harlequin Reader Service
P.O. Box 52040, Phoenix, AZ 85072-2040
Canadian address: P.O. Box 2800, Postal Station A,
5170 Yonge St., Willowdale, Ont. M2N 6J3

ALISON FRASER

a man worth knowing

Harlequin Books

TORONTO • NEW YORK • LONDON
AMSTERDAM • PARIS • SYDNEY • HAMBURG
STOCKHOLM • ATHENS • TOKYO • MILAN

Harlequin Presents first edition March 1986
ISBN 0-373-10865-6

Original hardcover edition published in 1985
by Mills & Boon Limited

CHAPTER ONE

KATE GREGORY glanced at her watch and gave up toying with her food.

'I'd better go and change,' she said with a heavy sigh.

'Hmm,' came the murmur from behind a book.

She rose from the table, not expecting more. The moment her brother Johnny became involved in a novel, he shut the world out.

Walking through to the other half of the room, she closed the folding partition that enabled their landlady to claim the place was a two-roomed flat.

The garden end was laid out as a tiny bedroom cluttered with a wardrobe, chest of drawers and double bed. None of the furniture matched and was made more incongruous by Mrs Karovski calling it antique. Only the woodworm in the wardrobe was old enough to qualify, Kate had thought at the time, but she'd not contradicted the landlady. Twelve months ago she'd been thankful to find a place she could afford.

She drew the curtains and switched on the light. A dress already lay on the bed. Of light green silk, it was cut in simple lines and suited her small, slender figure—but Kate was indifferent to how she looked: tonight's party would be duty rather than pleasure.

With her long hair coiled, she applied a pale lipstick and dusting of eyeshadow. Her lashes, the same jet black as her hair, didn't require emphasis to draw attention to large brown eyes, set in an otherwise delicate frame.

Ready in less than half an hour, she smiled as she made a final check in the mirror. Once she'd have spent as long selecting which dress to wear. Life had certainly changed.

'Tres chic,' Johnny announced on her return.

'Merci,' she acknowledged, wincing at his appalling pronunciation. 'I hope that's not all the French you've learned over the summer or Monsieur Cardin isn't going to be *tres enchanté* with you, Johnny.'

Grinning broadly, after a moment's consideration he offered, *'La plume de ma tante a liqué sur mon écris,'* as doubtful proof he had done some studying in the holidays.

'Brilliant ... for a *first* former,' Kate said in a dry tone for her brother was about to enter his 'O' level year. 'I'm frightened to ask what *"a liqué"* means.'

'Has leaked,' Johnny volunteered helpfully, and drew a grimace from Kate.

'Now I see what Monsieur Cardin referred to as your *inventive* approach to his language,' she groaned, quoting his last school report. 'How can you be so clever at maths and science, and so stupid at French?'

'Don't know,' he shrugged, obviously unworried by the fact. 'I guess my CPU didn't come equipped with language circuitry.'

'Your *what*?'

'My Central Processing Unit. Remember, that's the core of the computer which controls——'

'Yes, I remember,' Kate interrupted with a smile before Johnny could get into full swing. He had indeed explained the complexities of his school's computer— and at great length. Dutifully she had listened, lost after the first sentence or two of confusing buzzwords and endless intials, although giving a good pretence of fascination.

'Anyway you don't seem to have any problem learning computer languages,' she pointed out.

'It's hardly the same thing, Kate,' he returned with mild scorn. 'Basic and Fortran, they're precise and logical whereas French is——'

'—the "O" level language you'll need for university,' she inserted neatly.

Unable to deny it, he countered, 'I don't *have* to go to university.'

'No, you don't,' was agreed without argument for Kate knew an adolescent challenge when she heard one—and better than to meet it. Only six years older and not always wiser, she recognised the limits of her authority over her brother.

But he was a good boy, mostly. He never complained about their changed circumstances and he was more responsible than many his age.

When she began to clear up the supper dishes, he insisted he would tidy up later. Then he escorted her to the tube station at Holland Park—and, buying a platform ticket, waited with her among the Saturday night crowd.

'You'll take a taxi home.' It was an order, accompanied by a look that was meant to be stern.

'Yes, John.' Kate echoed his grave tone, suppressing a smile as she wondered, not for the first time, who was looking after whom in their relationship.

'And enjoy the party!' was added when a tube-train rattled into the station.

Another brotherly command but she wasn't giving any promises on that one. 'It's work really. Howard's paying me a bonus to see his farewell party goes smoothly.'

'That doesn't mean you won't——' he began to argue.

'I have to go,' Kate cut in hastily, kissing his cheek and dashing on board the tube.

But before the doors could close, a determined Johnny yelled after her, '—Meet someone nice!' and grinned from ear to ear as the train pulled away, leaving him with the last word.

His sister was half smiling when she turned to find several of her fellow passengers staring. Fortunately their interest was brief, quickly averted back to newspapers and magazines. But self-conscious, Kate took a seat at the farthest end of the carriage and occupied her mind with imagining the dire things she could do to Johnny when she got home. If she'd nagged him about his French revision over the summer, he'd done his fair share of driving her up the wall—in the name of what he saw as a worthy cause.

Recalling other holidays when there had been a steady stream of callers for his older sister, he believed she must be missing that time. She didn't think so.

With difficulty, she'd adjusted to living in the tiny,

shabby flat, sometimes hankering after aspects of their old life, but the young men who had pursued the girl she had once been, were mostly vague memories now. Another life.

Three stops later, she alighted at Lancaster Gate. Howard Carson, her employer, lived in an enormous Georgian house leased from a diplomat on a posting abroad. It was a lovely house, having all the elegance and charm of a more gracious age—Howard, unfortunately, had little of either!

'You're late, Kate honey,' he said the moment she came through the door, almost as if he had been waiting in the chequered hallway just to tell her so.

Counting to ten—the exact number of minutes she was in fact late—she slipped out of her coat and said tonelessly, 'Yes, I'm sorry.'

Howard looked on the verge of pursuing it and Kate was relieved he didn't. If he'd muttered his usual, 'Well, little lady, don't let it happen again,' she might have laughed aloud, considering this was her last night of working for the moody American writer. As it was, she felt she deserved a medal for enduring him for twelve very long months.

'Check on those goddamn caterers, Kate, will you?' he asked a shade more civilly. 'They seem useless to me.'

Those 'goddamn caterers' were some of the best in London, Kate knew. Howard was simply nervous—success hadn't come till his mid-thirties and, five years on, he still felt the need to impress people with it.

But Kate did as she was told.

It was to be a cocktail-cum-supper party. The buffet table in a room off the main lounge was faultless, its attendant chef immaculate in whites. She complimented him on the magnificent spread of delicacies and passed back through to the living room.

'Everything all right?' she enquired of the man setting up a well-stocked spirit bar for the evening.

'Yes, miss,' the barman smiled back. 'Provided they don't ask for anything too obscure—I can cope with the Harvey Wallbangers.'

'If that happens, let the guest mix it himself. I believe

it's an artistic hobby,' she said, giving him a conspiratorial wink that put him at his ease. Soon they would be swamped by Howard's friends, mainly compatriots from the world of ex-Broadway plays and musicals, other American writers also temporarily based in London, and even a few minor Embassy officials.

'Everything's fine,' she announced to Howard when he rejoined her in the hall, now dressed in an evening suit that slimmed down his heavy frame. A dark, rugged-featured man, he was considered attractive by some women, if not Kate.

'Swell,' he smiled, evidently in a better humour. 'Fix this, will you, Kate?'

She reached up to make a perfect bow of his black tie and he went on, 'I want you to stay close tonight.'

'What about Sylvia?' His current actress girlfriend would not like her constantly around.

'Sylvia's why I want you close,' he grinned.

'Oh.' It was a restrained murmur. Howard intended to use her to fend off another *ex*-girlfriend.

'You have more class anyway, baby.' He patted her cheek and she stiffened. 'Even if it's that prissy English variety. Beats me why a looker like you sticks at secretarial work.'

'Beats me too,' Kate thought in exasperation but censored it to, 'I enjoy it, Howard.'

She still hoped he might live up to his promise of finding her a job with one of his friends. And it wasn't a total lie. When Howard had concentrated on his book rather than on patronising her, some of the research he'd trusted her to do had been quite interesting.

'Well, you're damn good at it,' he acknowledged, a rare compliment on her actual work. 'And at organising this sort of affair. Where did you learn that—not in secretarial school?'

'No, my parents used to give parties,' she admitted reluctantly. Her mother's parties formed some of her earliest memories—lavish affairs that had seemed fascinating viewed from the balcony in Elmsfield Hall.

Howard squinted at her curiously when she did not add to her reply. 'So what happened?'

'They stopped giving parties,' Kate muttered back.

It took a long awkward moment for Howard to decide whether he was being snubbed or amused. Fortunately he made the wrong choice and laughed.

Then switching subjects, he asked, 'Thought any more about my offer?'

'No, I'm sorry—it's impossible,' she dismissed hastily. The offer in question had been generous—her air fare, increased salary and an apartment in one of the more upmarket areas of New York—but she wasn't altogether sure what Howard expected for his money.

She did, however, give him the benefit of the doubt by adding, 'But thanks all the same, Howard.'

'Your commitments, huh?' he repeated the vague excuse she'd already used. 'Well, honey, it's your decision but as far as I can see—this commitment of yours, *he* sure as hell isn't making you happy.'

Kate frowned, considering whether she should explain about Johnny. But the doorbell rang and Howard went on quickly, 'Listen, after the party gets going, perhaps we could find time for another little talk. Because I'd still like you to come back with me next week. In fact I'd more than like it . . . if you know what I mean.'

If Kate hadn't, his behaviour that night would have been a fairly adequate clue. But for the first couple of hours she tolerated his casual squeezes on her waist while skilfully eluding his arm as a permanent attachment.

From general dogsbody she suddenly seemed to have been promoted to his lady friend for the evening. Her only consolation was not being expected to contribute much to the conversation. While Howard responded to questions about his recently completed book, she contented herself with raising mental eyebrows at the lofty, literary terms he used. Entertaining his thrillers were—art they were not.

Then when Sylvia finally arrived, Kate lasted another quarter of an hour before deciding that Howard, at his brashest, deserved Sylvia, at her bitchiest.

Slipping away from the smoke and heat, Kate found the balcony empty and sat wearily down on one of the the chairs in the corner. She was tempted to slip away altogether but she couldn't risk offending Howard, not if he might recommend her as a secretary to one of his writer friends. So she resigned herself to returning to his side after a brief respite from the party's noise.

She could have groaned aloud when some minutes later her solitude was suddenly interrupted by a male voice asking, 'Mind if I sit down?'

Apart from a quick reflex glance, she made no effort to acknowledge the request. At any rate her unwelcome company was already settling himself in the patio chair beside hers, stretching his long legs on to the one opposite. Kate wasn't going to get the chance to mind.

'Feel free,' she muttered drily and continued to stare straight ahead. She was tired and tetchy, in no mood for party small talk.

'Fascinating, isn't it?' the newcomer eventually remarked.

Coming after a lengthy silence, it startled Kate into a bewildered, 'What is?'

'I don't know—you tell me,' was drawled back in an American accent underscored with amusement. 'I'm damned if I can see anything but pitch darkness out there.'

It might have been against her but, lips quirking, Kate saw the joke. Or did until she turned her head to take a good look at her companion under the balcony lighting. Although his features were not wholly familiar, his smile was. It rapidly wiped any trace of humour from her face.

'I'm afraid I don't talk to strangers,' she declared stonily, and immediately wished she hadn't. It made her sound about twelve years old.

'We have met,' he pointed out, his mouth still curved in that wry smile.

'I don't recall it,' she lied, after giving his face a further unnecessary inspection. She would have re-membered his eyes if nothing else.

They were an unusually deep blue, alight with the

same mockery they'd held that first time. The blond beard of a week ago had been shaved off to reveal strong, perfectly chiselled features and a deep tan— made more arresting by his fair colouring.

'And I thought we made rather an . . . *impact* on each other,' he chuckled, then laughed outright when she shot him a look intended to be crushing. 'Do you want any clues to jog your memory?'

'No, thank you,' she said coldly but it didn't stop him.

'I'll show you my bruises if you show me yours,' he suggested with a wicked grin, and for a second Kate imagined he was about to do precisely that as he bent one leg.

'Okay, I remember!' she snapped back.

Late for a dental appointment, she'd come hurtling down Howard's steps right into this stranger's arms as they both rounded the pillar on the street. That had been an accident; what followed hadn't.

'I simply don't wish to build on the acquaintance,' she continued in what Howard would call her prissy English tone, 'and I don't believe I hurt you in the slightest.'

His brow rose a fraction and he drawled back, 'Don't you now? Well, all I can say is you don't need any karate lessons to defend yourself, lady.'

Kate looked away from mocking blue eyes, feeling uncomfortable. And that was ridiculous. She'd every right to kick him. The conversation had been minimal. He'd steadied her, she'd offered a breathless apology and they'd stared at each other for a moment, embarrassed. Or at least she had been; he obviously didn't know the meaning of that word. His actions had proved that.

Now, as if her recollections had been out loud, he defended, 'It was just a kiss, after all.'

And if she was reading *him* correctly, she was being accused of having over-reacted. It took an effort to stop herself giving a repeat performance.

'Then could you possibly shut up about it?' she suggested icily, although there was the light of battle in her eyes when she recalled his 'just a kiss'. More like a full-blooded assault!

'I guess I got a little carried away,' he admitted, again picking up on her thoughts rather than her words, 'but there were extenuating circumstances.'

Sensing he was still laughing at her, Kate indulged her own humour, 'Don't tell me—a full moon brought out the wolf in you? Or maybe you go a little crazy when there's an "r" in the month?'—undiluted sarcasm at the memory of his head suddenly lowering towards her to blot out bright sunshine.

'Not so sweet Kate,' he responded musingly.

She scowled at his use of her name. Howard had asked her the next day if she had run into a tall blond guy and she assumed she had been discussed.

'But you're very pretty,' he added.

'Sorry?' The sudden compliment seemed totally out of context.

'The extenuating circumstance,' he explained glibly.

'Th-that's *it*?—that I'm p-pretty!' she stammered incredulously.

'All right, you're beautiful,' he conceded, deliberately misunderstanding her. 'Outstandingly so, if you want my humble opinion.'

Kate didn't. Acidly she returned, 'Am I expected to be flattered by it?'

A second's thought and he was shrugging casually, 'No, I guess the mirror tells you the same thing every morning.'

There was nothing casual, however, about the way his eyes slid from her face to her bare shoulders and the merest hint of cleavage offered by the square, thin-strapped neckline of her dress, then lingered where the silk outlined her small, rounded breasts. For a moment she was too shocked to speak, unable to believe any man, even this one, would be quite so blatant about his interest. He was on his way down to her legs by the time she found her voice again.

Refusing to show her embarrassment, she said as a biting putdown, 'Could I possibly have my dress back?'

'Sorry, was I being obvious?' He raised his head and Kate thought she had never seen a smile that was less apologetic. He had thoroughly enjoyed giving rein to his imagination and undeterred by her frigid stare, he murmured meaningfully, 'Howard has some beautiful things.'

'I hope that's a *non sequitur,*' she retorted furiously.

'I hope so too,' he agreed but with an interrogative lift to one brow.

Kate sensed Howard's heavy hand behind the half-question. It wouldn't be the first time he'd given the wrong impression to one of his 'buddies'. Well, she wasn't going to waste breath explaining herself—not to this wretched American, anyway. It was beneath her dignity.

'Do you want to hear what Howard told me about you?' he resumed softly.

'Not particularly,' she muttered, affecting boredom, 'but I don't suppose that will stop you.'

'The girl's beginning to know me,' he said, eyes lit with ready laughter.

And she was. Irritated as much by his unfailing humour as his persistence, she flipped back, 'Should I hope for any improvement?'

'Perhaps,' he said but his low chuckle made it seem doubtful. 'I'd better tell you what our mutual friend said before your curiosity overwhelms you.'

The worst of it was that he was right—she did want to know despite the conviction she wasn't going to like it one bit.

Adopting Howard's more exaggerated drawl he went on, 'Quote——"Her name's Kate. Ain't she goddamn something, boy?"—unquote.'

And Kate was just deciding it wasn't nearly as bad as she'd anticipated when a hand suddenly closed over hers, resting on a chair arm, and he added as an apparent afterthought, 'Oh yes, and I was to keep my hands off his property—or words to that effect.'

A flame of angry colour flooded Kate's face. Damn Howard Carson and his need to feed his ego at her expense.

'Then perhaps you should heed my lord and master,' she replied in a purely sarcastic vein as she stared at the large hand trapping hers.

To Kate's surprise, he obeyed almost instantly, giving her fingers a gentle squeeze before removing his hand altogether to reach into a shirt pocket for cigarettes. Offered one, she refused curtly, just as annoyed by his quick acceptance of Howard's rights. Had he taken her sarcasm seriously? From his next remark, it appeared he hadn't.

'I'd like to meet the man who could master you, sweet Kate,' he drawled when, cigarette lit, he raised his eyes to catch her glaring at him. 'And something tells me old Howie couldn't even make first base outside his imagination.'

Kate frowned at the unfamiliar Americanism. 'Does that mean you don't believe what Howard implied?' and at his nod, demanded, 'Why not?'

'Well,' he began, smiling despite her sharpness, 'I was trapped in a corner by a boy wonder from the Embassy, righting the world in ten easy moves, when I happened to look in your direction once or twice . . .'

'And?' she prompted, uncertain if she liked being watched.

'*And* you seemed less than thrilled by our host's little attentions towards you,' he said, clearly amused by the fact.

'Really.' It was a non-committal sound as Kate worried if he might pass his observation on to Howard.

Perhaps not for he volunteered, 'A word of advice though—if you want to discourage him, I'd forget the subtle approach. I suspect your cool superior ways are probably lost on poor old Howie.'

They were. But evidently not on this man, his lazy air deceptive. She began to wonder exactly which category of Howard's friends he fitted. He had the looks of an actor but none of the mannerisms; if he had any skills of diplomacy, they were well hidden; and cynically she assumed, as a writer, he would have mentioned his latest book by now. In fact from his weathered complexion and unruly, sun-bleached hair, he seemed more an outdoors type.

Whatever he was, he certainly didn't look as though a sophisticated London party was his normal scene. In white cotton shirt and jeans, he was dressed extremely casually compared with the other guests. Yet she doubted it would bother him, being out of step with the crowd. His self-confidence was no blustering camouflage like Howard's.

Made conscious by one of his slow, amused smiles that she was actually staring as hard as he had earlier, Kate covered the fact by asking, 'Are you a close friend of Howard's?'

'In ways,' he replied and had her heart sinking until he qualified, 'But then I've known him a long time—when he was a poorer but better man, you might say. And being the same sex, of course, I don't get treated to Howard's heavy snow techniques.'

'*Snow* techniques?' she echoed.

'Chatting up,' he translated after thought. 'Trying to get you into——'

'Never mind, I've got the picture!' she interrupted with a snap and he laughed softly at her primness.

Uncoiling his legs, he leaned forward to stub out his cigarette. Kate thought he might be preparing to leave. But no such luck. Instead he scraped his chair nearer.

'So what sort of reference did I get from Howie?' he asked after they traded glances, his interested, hers more wary than hostile now. 'Not good, at any rate.'

'I didn't ask,' she said truthfully.

Howard himself had volunteered a few remarks and if *Howard* called him bad news for good girls, *well* . . .

'The girl has no curiosity,' he murmured in disbelief. 'Or maybe total strangers make a habit of kissing her.'

'All the time,' she replied flippantly. 'I've lost count.'

He laughed aloud and it was a deep pleasant sound that had Kate unbending enough to smile back. Impossible to stay aloof from someone who took nothing seriously, least of all himself.

He was quick to make capital of her lapse. 'I'd better introduce myself if we're going to be friends.'

Her uncompromising, 'We're not,' was totally ignored.

'Michael Sullivan Fitzgerald, but you may call me
Van for short.'

'Thanks,' she muttered with heavy irony, only to be
thrown completely by his next action. Stupidly she
stared at the hand outstretched towards her until she
realised she was meant to take it.

His handshake was brief but firm, and Kate was
dazed by the leap from the middle of a conversation to
a politely formal beginning. She stopped thinking him
different, and started thinking him a little crazy. Then
asked herself why she was still sitting here, listening to
him, when she should be inside, keeping in Howard's
good books.

And with that in mind, she rose abruptly to her feet,
hoping he would take the hint. But he followed
immediately, broader and taller than she remembered.

'Are we going back to the party?' he enquired
blandly.

'*I* am,' she stressed, waiting for him to get out of her
way.

'Pity,' he returned smoothly, 'I thought we were
building rather nicely on the acquaintance.'

'Strange,' she rallied more sarcastically, 'I thought we
were working backwards and we'd just come to the end
of your *line*.'

It was to have been a parting shot but Kate spent a
second too long savouring the slip in his smile. By the
time she brushed past him, he'd recovered, making a
grab for her arm to stop her short.

'Okay—I was moving a little too fast,' he said before
she could pull away.

Kate detected no humour for once. 'Is that meant to
be an apology?' she returned stiffly.

There was a noticeable silence before he conceded,
'Yeah, I guess so.' From his tone it was clear he didn't
make a habit of apologising for his behaviour and knew
it himself, for he added, 'Not the most gracious,
maybe.'

But the only one she was going to get, Kate realised
as she murmured, 'It'll do.'

They stared at each other for a moment longer and

Kate felt his hold relaxing, his fingers brushing lightly where they might have bruised. Not an unpleasant sensation but she shivered all the same.

'You're cold. Come on,' he said with another quick smile, 'we'd better go in again.'

Hand at her elbow, he guided her ahead of him and it wasn't until they reached the patio doors that Kate was quite certain he was favouring his left leg. She had thought his sense of humour more subtle.

'I don't find that funny,' she said, rounding on him to find his frown of incomprehension even more irritating. With a withering look, she listed, 'First, I had every right to kick you, second, you shouldn't fake that sort of thing, and last—it was the *other* leg!'

He'd folded his arms, adopting an attitude of amused patience. When she finished, he commented succinctly, 'You had, one shouldn't, and it was.'

It took Kate several seconds to unravel his answer and longer to quite take it in. 'Did you just agree with me?' she demanded, obviously put out by the idea.

'Yeah, but I don't count on it being a regular feature of our relationship,' he quipped, mocking her quick temper, but when she showed signs of losing it again, he held up his hands in a gesture of submission and reverted to seriousness so there was no further misunderstanding. 'My limp is real, I'm afraid.'

A soundless, mortified, 'Oh,' was all Kate's lips could form but her eyes said more.

'Don't go soft on me, Kate,' he jibed, reading the compassion in them. 'I was just beginning to enjoy the fight.'

'I . . . I . . .' She dropped her gaze from his.

'And don't let it bother you,' he said with a cooler edge to his voice.

'It doesn't,' Kate denied quickly. 'I was surprised, that's all. You look athletic.'

She met his eyes again and waited to see if her unusual gaucheness was to be forgiven. It was.

'I don't let it slow me up,' he murmured insinuatingly.

'I had noticed,' she returned, more pert than prim

and suddenly they smiled together. And just as suddenly Kate felt a small pull of attraction increase to a sharp, alarming tug.

She sensed he was about to reach out for her and she wasn't certain how she'd react. Unwisely, she suspected. So it was probably fortunate the unpredictable English climate took the decision from her as a light drizzle began and forced them inside.

CHAPTER TWO

'GOD, it's worse than when we left,' Van said as the first wave of noise and heat hit them. Then he bent his head closer to hers to murmur, 'We could go back out to the balcony . . . I'll risk it if you will.'

He was teasing again. Or Kate supposed he was from the wicked gleam in his eye, too staged to be real. *He'd* risk it indeed! She didn't think he was referring to the rain.

Hiding a smile, she looked away and he added with an amused groan, 'Too late—seems we're about to have company.'

Frowning, Kate spotted Howard threading through the crowd—Sylvia in tow. Their progress was delayed by greetings from other guests but Kate knew it was a temporary reprieve when she caught Howard's heavy glances in her direction. With a grimace, she realised it would probably be sensible to return to his side, suitably apologetic for her absence.

Only before she could put the idea into action, a hand was grasping hers and the next thing she knew, she was being pulled round the edge of the party, out into the empty hall beyond. She had no real chance to protest until Van Fitzgerald closed the lounge door behind them.

'What do you think you're doing?' she demanded, after she wrenched her hand from his.

'Rescuing you from Howard, I assumed.'

Evidently he'd expected her to be pleased by his action. Was he too stupid to understand that in her position as an employee rather than guest, she couldn't afford to cut Howard dead like that?

'Then you assumed wrongly!' she muttered caustically as he tried a smile on her. 'For one, I don't enjoy being hauled across a room full of people and for another, I am perfectly capable of handling Howard without you playing Sir Galahad and making things a damn sight worse.'

Kate's voice was so sarcastic any other man would have either shouted back—or made a hasty retreat. Not Van Fitzgerald. He simply stood there, head at an angle, listening as though fascinated. Then remarked, with what sounded suspiciously like amusement, 'You know for a cool English lady, you've quite a temper, Kate honey.'

'*Don't* call me honey!' hissed Kate, barely in control of that temper.' *And* get out of my way!'

'Okay, okay.' He took a step backwards. 'And I won't call you honey again. But calm down, Kate, will you?'

His soft drawl was so reasonable, so damn patronising, Kate wanted to scream. Somehow she restrained herself to a smothered groan of frustration before turning away altogether and crossing towards the hall telephone.

She'd had enough of Howard's party and Howard's friends. She would come back on Monday for her bonus. And if he complained about her leaving early, she could always tell him Fitzgerald had been bothering her. It was true, after all. By the time she'd finished ordering a mini-cab, Van was sitting on the other side of the stair railing from the telephone table.

'Going home?' he asked with a smile.

He really was very good at understatement, Kate conceded. Or was she reading the words 'running away' into the quiet question? She limited herself to a cold stare, and, heels clicking across the marble floor, she retrieved her coat from the hallstand.

She intended to wait on the front steps but she'd forgotten the rain, now driving down in a heavy sheet.

He hadn't.

'Good old British weather,' he commented when she slipped back inside.

He was still seated on the stairs and Kate felt as long as he stayed his distance, she could ignore him. She should have known better.

The mini-cab had been promised within twenty minutes. After ten spent standing in a corner by the door, sensing him watching her as if she were a prize exhibit in London zoo and listening to his low tuneless whistle, her nerves were at snapping point.

'Why don't you go back to the party?' she eventually demanded, then at the glimmer of satisfaction in his eyes, regretted being the first to break.

He shrugged. 'I hate parties—that sort anyway.'

'What sort?' Kate retorted, having spent the best part of her morning arranging the party so casually dismissed.

'You know—all caviare and phoney conversation,' he drawled back.

Kate didn't exactly disagree with the judgment but she asked sharply, 'Why did you come then?'

'Well, I thought a certain English girl might be going to it,' he admitted with a laugh. 'And she might let me take her on somewhere else—"far from the madding crowd", as it were.'

'That was arrogant of you,' she stated derisively.

'Not really,' he denied, relaxing back against the stairs to survey her from head to toe and bringing another blush to her cheeks. 'Let's just say optimistic.'

'Very!' Kate scoffed. 'I'm not that sort of girl.'

'What sort?' he asked blandly, eyes full of laughter.

He received a frigid look in return. 'The sort that lets herself be taken *somewhere else* after parties.'

'Point made.' He inclined his head, mocking her regal tone.

'Good!' she snapped.

'But—for the record—I was considering a quiet wine bar where we could talk,' he jeered softly, and smile back in place, went on, 'What did you have in mind? It sounds much more interesting.'

Finally lost for words, Kate wished the condition had occurred earlier. Somehow he'd turned the conversation to make her seem the one being arrogant in assuming he was propositioning her. The very casualness of his manner suggested she had been and she stood tongue-tied, as a minute ticked by on the hallway clock.

'Okay, I'll settle for the wine bar,' he murmured, relieving her of what he must know was an embarrassed silence.

'I'm not sure.' She was surprised to find herself wavering.

'I'll be good,' he promised, crossing his heart but cancelling the effect with a devilish smile.

'He's unstoppable,' Kate thought, but with all the charm Howard lacked. Yet if she saw the attraction he would hold for many women, she'd be crazy to fall for it.

In the end her sanity was not put to the test. While a patient Van Fitzgerald waited for her answer, a very impatient Howard came bursting into the hall. Noticing her first, he closed the door behind him.

With a silent groan, Kate wondered how Howard was going to behave. Badly, she did not doubt.

But when she gave him a look of appeal, it was answered with a smile—or perhaps leer would have been a more accurate description.

'You're not leaving, Kate baby, are you?' he asked as he walked towards her, a sway in his step. 'We were going to have a little talk, remember?'

Kate was confused. She remembered all right but from the way Howard's eyes were running over her, *talking* was the last thing in his mind. Surely he wasn't going to make a pass at her in front of Fitzgerald?

She glanced past Howard's shoulder to the other American, lounging on the stairs, a grin on his face, and it suddenly struck her. Howard hadn't seen him—and *he* wasn't about to announce his presence.

'*Howard!*' she hissed in warning, but Howard was oblivious.

When Kate raised her hands to fend him off, he coaxed, 'Aw, come on, Kate. Be nice, huh? After all,

I've been good to you, haven't I? And I could be even better if——'

'*Howard, please!*' Kate found herself backed into a corner, and tried distracting him with, 'Listen, where's Sylvia? Won't she be wondering what's happened to you?'

'Sylvia? You're not jealous of her, Kate baby?' he suggested and left Kate wide-eyed at his conceit. 'You know it's you I'm interested in.'

Kate began to shake her head as Howard leaned towards her, whisky fumes on his breath. 'Sure you do,' he slurred, placing a heavy hand on her shoulder. 'And maybe you like old Howie a little—'cos you got rid of Van, didn't you?'

'I'm afraid not.' A third voice entered the conversation just as Kate started to twist away, more nauseated than frightened.

It was almost comic the way Howard froze, then dropped his jaw, and finally spun round, rocking on his feet. Only Kate wasn't in the mood to laugh. In fact she wasn't even sure if she felt that grateful to Fitzgerald. He might have rescued her but he had taken his own sweet time about it.

'Van! I didn't see you there . . .' A flustered Howard stated the obvious.

'I'd gathered that,' was replied as the other man levered himself from the stairs. 'I thought I'd better interrupt before you got too carried away. You haven't changed much, have you, *old Howie?*'

Howard's eyes narrowed slightly but if he noticed the careless contempt in his friend's tone, he decided to ignore it, grinning back. 'I still like a pretty woman, if that's what you mean, Van boy.'

'Kate's not pretty—she's beautiful,' he was corrected in a deadpan voice. 'And actually I meant you were still about as subtle as a Sherman tank.'

Kate shut her eyes in silent despair. What was Fitzgerald trying to do—provoke Howard more?

'Yeah, well . . .' Howard muttered, a flush spreading over his blunt features, 'the little lady here might have told me you were around, 'stead of leading me on.'

Kate's eyes flew open in stunned disbelief. But not wanting to make the situation any worse, she managed to keep silent. Unfortunately, Van had no such reservations.

'Leading you on?' he repeated with a short, derisive laugh. 'Hell, Howard, from where I was sitting, seems to me she was fighting you off. So why don't you leave her alone, mm?'

Howard's flush deepened. He wasn't so drunk, he didn't appreciate he had made a fool of himself. But he was drunk enough to resent it—and the almost possessive attitude Van was showing towards Kate. 'Leave her alone, and let you take over, maybe?' he challenged thickly.

'That's up to her,' Van dismissed himself from the issue. 'Just so long as you understand, she doesn't return your *interest* . . . Do you, Kate?'

'I——' Kate's eyes moved nervously between the men. Van was smiling at her, confident he was right—and of course he was. But Howard was giving her a mean look that warned her exactly where her interests did lie.

She thought of the forty pounds she had yet to receive, the possible recommendation Howard would make to one of his friends, and felt a traitor in saying, 'Please stay out of this, Mr Fitzgerald.'

'You heard the lady,' Howard crowed with satisfaction.

'Yeah, I heard her,' Van echoed, his gaze fixed on Kate, questioning where all that earlier pride had gone.

She looked away.

'Obviously doesn't return your interest either, old buddy.' Howard laughed unpleasantly. 'Perhaps you're not the man you were, Van—in more ways than one.'

Kate flinched at the cruel jibe but its target showed little reaction apart from taking a couple of steps nearer, as if to draw attention to his limp.

'Perhaps you'd like to find out, Howard,' he countered coolly.

'Hey, Van——' Howard spread his arms in appeal, 'I was only joking, old buddy.'

'I'm not laughing, Howard.' The gap was closed some more.

And suddenly Kate recognised that he was, in fact, deadly serious. His hands were clenchèd in fists by his sides, those blue eyes measuring the distance between Howard and himself. She wasn't quite sure why he was ready to fight—for his pride or hers—but either way it seemed madness. Even without his disability, he must be thirty pounds lighter than Howard's brawling frame.

'Howard.' She reached for his arm, desperately trying to defuse the atmosphere. 'Listen, I've got to go home. I'll come back on Monday if you want but can I have my money now . . . please.'

Kate wanted to make sure she at least got paid, as promised. Howard certainly didn't look too happy about her request. Things weren't going as he'd planned. But when he glanced at Van, something in the other man's expression changed his mind.

'Sure, honey.' He brought out his wallet and made a performance of counting out some crisp ten pound notes. 'Forty as agreed and another ten for doing a good job earlier.'

'Thanks, Howard.' She managed to sound grateful but he didn't hand the money over immediately. Instead he fanned it between his fingers.

'She works for you?' Van interrupted the little charade. 'You didn't tell me that,' he added, directing a frown at Kate.

She didn't know what he expected her to say. She'd assumed he knew she was Howard's secretary and she couldn't see any reason to defend the fact.

It was Howard who answered for them both, if rather cryptically. 'Come on, Van, there are certain things people don't advertise.'

'What do you mean?' was demanded in reply.

'What do you think I mean, Van?' Howard said with a smirk.

But whatever he *was* thinking made Van Fitzgerald shake his head in denial.

''Fraid so, boy,' Howard continued, his normal brash

confidence restored. 'As you said, I haven't changed that much. Success has merely improved my taste.'

Van's eyes shifted to a perplexed Kate. They ran over her sleek black hair, the refined beauty of her features, before he muttered harshly, 'You're lying.'

'Classy, isn't she?' Howard cupped her chin but removed his hand before she could protest. 'Kate's the best little hostess around. Aren't you, baby?'

'You're lying!' Van repeated through clenched teeth though his eyes switched back to Kate, questioning her shrug at the compliment.

'Maybe.' Howard waved the notes in his hand. 'Why don't you ask the *lady* if she pays tax on her money?'

'*Howard!*' Kate pleaded, coming to life as this last remark made the rest of their confusing dialogue seem irrelevant.

'Do you?' Van shot at her.

'I . . .' She hesitated, guilt written all over her face. After her first month Howard had suggested paying her in cash and saving them both the trouble of filling out tax forms. He'd made it seem a small matter but she'd known it to be wrong—which only made it more wrong that she'd agreed.

'Do you?' was demanded once again at her silence.

'I . . . No. No, I don't,' she admitted in a small voice.

'I'm sure you can add two and two, Van?' Howard drawled, highly amused by whatever was going on. 'Here, honey.' He held out the money to her.

'Damn you, Kate!' the other American swore as she went to take it. 'Tell me the bastard's lying.'

She stared back at him, her actions frozen. His eyes were blazing with anger. He looked as if he'd attack *her* now if she so much as touched the money. She could scarcely believe her dishonesty was making him this furious.

Ashamed she mumbled, 'It's not your concern,' and lost what little composure she had left when Howard began to laugh.

She took the money and literally ran—through the door, leaving it flung wide, and out into the night. She paused for a second at the foot of the steps, and then raced along the rain-washed pavement, hearing the splash of running footsteps behind. If her high heels hadn't made her frightened of slipping, she might have been certain of escape for it wasn't Howard pursuing. As it was, they both almost fell over when Fitzgerald eventually caught up and made a clumsy grab for her.

'Let me go!' she cried as she was spun round to face him.

For moments he said nothing. Did nothing. Just stared at her as the rain beat down on them, plastering hair to skin, soaking through clothes, streaming down their faces. Anger and disbelief in his eyes, bewilderment in hers. Then something inside him seemed to snap.

'Why the hell didn't you tell me before?' he yelled at her.

'Tell you what?'

'About this!' And he squeezed her wrist so hard she opened her hand.

'My money!' She watched it flutter to the ground.

'You'd get down in the gutter after it, wouldn't you?' he spat out as he prevented her doing precisely that.

'I need it!' she screamed back, twisting frantically out of his arms but too late to do anything about the notes washed away by the driving rain into the nearest drain.

'That's what they all say.' He dragged her to him again. 'Only you're no two-bit street hooker who doesn't know any better.'

'Hooker?' she repeated slowly before realising how much slower she'd been inside the house.

'Hostess then, or call girl—or whatever damn fancy name you use for selling it!' he enlarged, shouting above the rain.

'Why you——' In blind fury, Kate took a swipe at him, then followed it up by slapping and punching and kicking—anything that might hurt him back.

But even with her striking out wildly, the American showed reluctance to use his strength to more than restrain her until finally his hold slackened on a sharp note of pain. Not thinking about it, Kate pushed him as hard as she could, and if she heard the clatter of dustbins behind her, she didn't stop to look back.

She ran out into the road and narrowly missed a passing car. It screeched to a halt and she saw its taxi sign on the roof. When the driver rolled down his window to yell at her, she jumped in first, 'I think I'm your fare,' and before he could argue, pleaded, 'Can I get in?'

The driver looked at her face, tears now streaming alongside the rain, and gave her a curious stare before nodding.

'Elgin Terrace,' she urged on climbing inside.

'You all right, love?'

'Yes, fine.' She caught a sob in her throat. 'Just drive on—*please*.'

The driver shrugged, swivelled back in his seat and made a U-turn in the wide street.

Kate rested her head against the seat and still didn't look back. She hoped he'd broken his neck, but anger didn't stop her tears. Sniffing, she searched her bag for a handkerchief. The car halted at some lights and she caught the driver's eye in the mirror. Mercifully he proved the silent type and contented himself with staring.

She must look a mess. Like a lady of the night, she thought, only the humour fell flat on her. How could he have believed *that* of her? She shut her eyes and tried to blank out the scene from her mind.

When she arrived home, she scrubbed at her tear-stained face before letting herself into the flat. Relieved the lights were out, she tiptoed in darkness to the far end of the room.

Johnny was stretched out on the bed asleep, all legs and arms, growing up fast. But still vulnerable in her eyes. Worth every day of the year working for Howard Carson, worth swallowing her pride for, worth even its humiliating end. Her baby brother—sometimes silly, always lovable. Well, perhaps not *always*. She managed a smile, remembering back to the first time she'd ever seen him . . .

In *her* nursery, a tiny thing with a mop of black hair and a wrinkled face. Smaller than her best doll and a lot less interesting—didn't talk like Amanda, didn't even open its eyes. Couldn't do anything but cry. Just deciding she hated him when Mama came in. Rustle of silk, scent of jasmine.

'Isn't your brother gorgeous, Katerina?' she cried and kissed her fingers to place them on the baby's forehead.

Definitely hated him.

'Yes, Mama.'

Kate always agreed with Mama.

'Would you like to feed him, madame? His bottle's ready,' the new nurse suggested.

'To be honest with you, Nanny,' Mama went on in a hushed voice, 'I find babies a trifle boring.'

Wasn't meant to hear that.

Still asked, 'Do *I* bore you, Mama?'

Made her laugh.

'Silly girl.' Mama kissed *her* properly. '*Je t'aime, ma petite.*'

Smiled. Knew what that meant. Mama often said nice things in French. Told her stories sometimes about her childhood in Paris and her Russian parents who had died in exile there.

'Your mother was saying she loves you very much,' Nanny said when Mama left.

Scowled. Didn't like *her*.

Muttered, 'Mama didn't say "very much". That's *je t'aime bien.*'

Got told off for being rude. Didn't care.

Baby stopped crying after it was fed. Nanny let her hold him for a second on her lap. Grinned at her. Decided not to hate him after all.

Knew now Mama wasn't going to love him any more than her . . .

And years later, Kate could see the irony of that small girl's thoughts—for in retrospect, Yelena St Gregory had been shallow, selfish and utterly vain. A beautiful woman, an enchanting woman in ways, but incapable of the love her young daughter had craved.

With black hair and dark almond-shaped eyes like her mother's, Kate had been petted and paraded for house guests in the holidays, largely ignored during term-time. She learned not to expect her mother to remember every school play or open day, and was heartbreakingly delighted when she did turn up, however late. Only once had she almost stopped loving her, when she waited three hours, forgotten on a station platform on a wintry December day. But her mother had made it up to her: at eleven, Kate had still believed presents were tokens of love.

Yet if a young Kate could forgive her mother anything, not so her father. Looking down at her sleeping brother, she traced the same strong lines on which Charles St Gregory's face had been modelled. A handsome man, she imagined her mother might have loved him once. She herself had never been able to love him at all.

Where her mother's interest had been erratic, his was non-existent. As a child Kate had sensed it and respected the distance he kept. By the time she was in her late teens she'd heard the words 'too busy', too many times, not to know it for a fact.

She had left school the daughter of rich parents, with no plans formed and no guidance given.

So she'd simply accepted that, being her mother's daughter, she was supposed to be happy flitting between fads and fancies, parties and long hours of idle gossip. Initially she'd tried. Actually wanted to be like her mother. Sought after, surrounded by admirers, captivating yet remaining elusive.

And she had been a success if one counted party invitations and willing escorts and earnest proposals from suitable young men. She should have been happy.

But as a year passed and a second began, she grew more and more dissatisfied. The days ran together. The suitable young men became indistinguishable with their talk of horses, yachts and cars. And she wasn't happy at all.

She supposed it had been foolish to go looking for direction from her father. But he was an intelligent man. Didn't everybody say so?—a financial wizard. And he had begun to show her some attention that second year, trusting her to act as a messenger for him at times. Admittedly her role was limited to delivering packages and the occasional briefcase to some business contact, and typically her father had not deigned to explain their contents, but some of these errands took her as far as Europe and she sensed they were at least important to him.

So one day she'd entered his study and stood patiently in front of his desk, waiting for an audience. Eventually he'd glanced up from his papers, surprise quickly followed by irritation. She recalled the conversation word for word.

'Father, I want to do something with my life,' she announced.

Slightly high-minded, perhaps, for the girl she was, but she hoped for once it would bring some reaction. A flicker of interest at least. Even his dry humour.

Silence.

She tried again. 'Maybe I could help you more . . , in the business, I mean.'

That tentative suggestion drew one word. 'No.'

A very final word which gave her the nerve to continue more stubbornly. 'Then I'd like to find a job, Father. I'm bored.'

'I thought you were going to Paris with your mother next week,' he said as if to settle the matter.

But she persisted, muttering, 'I can't go to fashion shows for the rest of my life.'

Now that got a reaction—his coldest stare. 'Are you being facetious, Katherine?'

'No, Father,' she mumbled, losing her nerve.

Appeased, he gave her future a moment's consideration and said quietly, 'I see no point in any such venture. You'll be getting married next year.'

Married? Kate repeated silently and watched as he bent his head again to the papers on his desk. Matter definitely settled.

She wasn't engaged, hadn't even formed a serious attachment to any of the boys she dated, yet she would be getting married next year. Her father really was a wizard: he could see into the future. She started to laugh, a shade hysterically. She regained his attention, more than usual.

'Katherine!' Half-reprimand, half-shock.

And then she was babbling like the idiot her father always made her feel.

'Don't tell me. You're busy. I can see that. I won't bother you again. *Ever* again!'

She'd kept her word too, Kate recalled. Not very difficult in the circumstances for while she stayed sulking at home, her father had gone to Paris with her mother. And there they had both died, victims of a hotel fire, only four days after Kate's little outburst.

Her wish for change had been granted.

CHAPTER THREE

KATE gave a low groan as the curtains were yanked open in one energetic sweep.

'An' sure and all, 'tis a beautiful morning,' her brother announced in a thick Irish accent: he was a good mimic though his audience was in no state to appreciate it.

'And the top of the morning to you too, little brother,' was replied in a much drier tone while eyes were screwed shut against the sudden light.

'Good party, eh?' Johnny bounced down on the narrow sofa-bed to receive an incoherent mumble. 'Was that yes or no?'

'Neither.' Blearily Kate opened her eyes again to register his broad grin. 'It was a protest against life in general and noisy little brothers in particular.'

'Grouch,' he accused.

'Pest.' She pulled a face back, and rubbing the sleep from her eyes, asked, 'What time is it?'

'Twelve,' her brother supplied and grinned when it had the desired affect.

'It can't be!' exclaimed Kate, brought bolt upright on the sofa bed.

And shamelessly Johnny admitted, 'No, actually it isn't,' but only after he was halfway to the door. 'I'm going for some milk. See you get out of bed the right side, sister dear.'

She threw a pillow and he ducked out of the door, laughing. She groped for her alarm clock to discover it was a few minutes past ten. Late enough.

She dressed hurriedly in dark red cords and a summer blouse trimmed with broderie anglaise, wondering how to spend the day. In the evening Johnny would be catching a train back to his school near Ipswich; she'd wanted to treat him this last afternoon to a restaurant lunch and a boat trip down the Thames but now, with no prospect of a job and barely money to see herself through the next week or two, she simply hadn't the cash. That fifty pounds would have made all the difference.

'Damn the man!' she swore as once more the image of a tall, blond American had her swallowing down anger. Why had he interfered, allowing Howard Carson to make fools of them both? She didn't credit that initially he'd called Howard a liar; in the end he'd been convinced, literally shouted the other man's insinuations at her above the rain.

'Lucky it's already got a crack in it,' her brother said, returning to catch her fierce scowl in the mirror.

'Charming,' she muttered back and with a last brush at her swathe of black hair, she took the milk bottle from his hand. Leaving him to bury his nose in a magazine, she went through to do battle with the gas cooker.

It was temperamental—or perhaps, this morning, she was. At any rate, she finally gave up on the lighter attachment and resorted to matches, shoving the grill pan in place with unnecessary force. The same annoyance was vented on the crockery as she slammed two cups on the formica worktop.

Surely she'd lost enough sleep last night without ruining today by dwelling on it? She couldn't change what had happened. She'd survived worse—*much* worse. And maybe Fitzgerald himself was feeling a little sick about his mistake. Or would he have laughed when Howard explained his nasty joke?

'Blast!' she swore again at the smell of burning toast. Disgusted with herself, she tossed the four blackened squares into the pedal bin and concentrated on what she was doing.

But later, when she was seated, cradling a cup of coffee in one hand and plucking at her chair's stuffing with the other, it was difficult not to brood about the future. If she didn't find a job within the next fortnight, even this shabby flat would be beyond her means. And no matter how desperate she was, she couldn't claim any state benefits. Her tax evasion was stupid as well as illegal, she now realised. Much too late to have qualms, she wondered if dishonesty could be an inherited trait. Sobering thought. What else would *she* do for money?

'Certainly not what?' Her brother was startled out of his thoughts, making Kate aware she had spoken her own aloud.

'Nothing,' she said quickly. 'I was talking to myself.'

'First sign of——'

'Yes, I know,' she cut in. 'Just start worrying when I answer myself back.'

'What were you thinking about? You sounded really angry.'

'Things,' she replied vaguely.

'What sort of things?'

'Oh, this and that.'

'Last night?' Johnny suggested, tossing away his magazine and sitting up.

'Last night? . . . the party, you mean,' she said as though she hadn't given it a thought.

'What was it like?' He came full circle back to the first question of the day.

'So-so,' she murmured non-committally but Johnny wasn't to be deflected.

'Anyone . . . interesting at it?' he asked next.

'Some writers, not as successful as Howard naturally,' she laughed. 'Oh, and several actors from American plays running in London.'

She offered him some of the more famous names but

he looked less than impressed—his heroes were mainly rugby players and athletes.

'Meet anybody . . . special then?' he pursued.

Johnny was still too young to give a convincing pretence of nonchalance. Kate smiled at his determined efforts though.

''Fraid not. Robert Redford couldn't make it,' she said with a sigh, 'and Sylvester Stallone had the bad taste to prefer blondes.'

'Sylvester Stallone was there!'

Apparently actors who played boxers rated much higher in adolescent eyes. One look at her brother's gullible, awestruck expression and Kate gave the game away by laughing.

He looked little boy cross and she jeered, 'Had you there, baby brother.'

'No, you didn't!'

'Yes, I did!'

'No, you . . .'

'Okay, okay,' she surrendered the argument before it began in earnest, and while she still had him distracted, changed the subject. 'Let's go out for a walk.'

'Where?'

'I don't know,' she shrugged. The sun was streaming through the front and back windows of the flat, highlighting every defect from worn carpet to cracked ceiling. Anywhere would do.

'The park,' she suggested.

'Hyde Park,' he stated his preference.

Kate had in mind a leisurely stroll to the nearest green area, Holland Park, not a forced march up the Bayswater Road, but she gave in. 'All right, although we'll have to watch the time.'

He stopped on their way to the front door. 'Hold it a sec'. I've forgotten something.'

She waited for him in the hall and groaned when she saw what he was carrying. 'Oh no, not that freebie thing.'

'Frisbee,' he corrected with a grin. 'You'd enjoy it if only you could get the hang of it,' he added and was awarded a very doubtful look in reply.

They walked up to Notting Hill Gate, busy even on a Sunday, and then cut through Kensington Gardens to the Serpentine. London was having a late summer between thunderstorms, and she felt hot and bothered by the time they came to rest beside the water's edge. She joined Johnny in slipping off her sandals and wriggling her toes in the cool water. She could have happily sat there all afternoon, watching the occasional rowing boat pass, but her brother seldom settled in one place for long.

They were deep into Hyde Park by the time they found a clear space away from picnics and Sunday footballers but she managed to throw herself into the game with some enthusiasm, if little skill. However, after an hour of retrieving the frisbee from wherever it landed—never in her hand despite Johnny's good aim—she was more than ready to admit defeat. Particularly as her grinning audience had augmented to include a Japanese boy who'd strolled over to watch them. Picking up the loathed disk, she tossed it to the newcomer and retired to flop down in the shade of a tree. Soon they had a fast, furious game going and Kate drowsed contentedly in the sun, still tired from her restless night.

The next thing she knew, Johnny was gently shaking her by the shoulder. 'Wake up, lazybones!'

She focused on him sleepily, then scanned the clearing. 'Where's your friend?'

'His parents dragged him away,' he sighed.

'Never mind, it's probably time we were getting back anyway,' she said, checking her watch. 'We have all your packing to do yet.'

'That won't take long.' Johnny shrugged, to be given a look of fond exasperation by Kate. From experience she knew his idea of packing was to transfer his clothes from wardrobe to suitcase in one heaped mass.

'By your method, maybe,' she murmured, standing up to brush her cords. 'Hungry?'

'Oh, I can hold off till supper at school,' she was assured quickly—too quickly, Kate judged and laughed. 'What's so funny?' he demanded.

'Well, I was going to buy you a hamburger and chips and a strawberry milkshake,' she said, smirking, 'but since you're not that hungry . . .'

If he hadn't been before, he certainly was now, after he'd been tempted with something other than her own culinary efforts. She wasn't offended—she cooked as badly as she frisbied—but she enjoyed teasing him.

'I am a little,' he admitted with a long face.

'A little?' she taunted.

'Okay, a lot,' he said when his stomach gave a betraying rumble. 'I didn't want to put you to any bother, that's all.'

'How thoughtful,' Kate commented wryly but done tormenting him, she reached into her pockets for some money. A few pounds wasn't going to halt any tide of misfortune. 'Run and get it, and I'll meet you at Lancaster Gate.'

She shook her head when he asked if she wanted anything, and he loped off, long co-ordinated strides taking him quickly over the grassy slopes. Kate adopted a more sedate pace. It really was warm and she veered away from the main pathways to the more shaded areas of the park.

Head bent in thought, she was just leaving the trees when a small ball suddenly appeared at her feet. Some reflex made her stoop to pick it up and she was hailed with a plaintive cry of, 'Pitch it, honey,' followed by the urgent direction, 'This way!'

She looked up, half-expecting to see a youth yelling for his cricket ball. Instead there was a figure, gesticulating wildly between wheezes. Although dressed in teenage clothing, he was balding and plumply middle-aged. The incongruous sight delayed Kate's reactions, and by the time she threw the ball, her catcher seemed to have lost interest and crumpled to his knees.

In the distance there was a minor roar of triumph and she came closer to view the rest of the field. Not cricket, she realised, but certainly another lunatic male game. Good-humoured catcalls from his own team got the fielder on his feet again, and he shambled off with a brief wave to Kate.

Unlike Johnny, she had little interest in sport but she slowed to watch on the far edge of the impromptu baseball court. It was really more spectacle than sport, comic and quite delightful, the players a mixture of ages from six to sixty.

From the distance most of the men seemed to be carrying extra weight under baggy sweatshirts. Somehow that made it nicer they were out here playing a game of their youth, not caring if they looked a little foolish.

There was only one whose build was at all athletic. He was wearing a sleeveless vest and denims, and from the back, his powerful shoulder muscles moved cleanly as he pitched the ball once more to the cry of, 'Strike!' when it was missed by the boy now on the batting line.

Kate thought it rather unfair he had what seemed the easiest job. But after he moved she had to revise that opinion. The man strolling forward to the young batsman had a noticeable limp which probably excluded him from a more energetic role.

When he eventually backed to the pitcher's spot, whatever advice he'd given the boy paid off as club hit ball with a resounding crack, sending it high and wide to scatter the fielders. Kate applauded with the other spectators, unaware that one pair of eyes was no longer on the delighted youngster, whooping round the circle.

The blue eyes in question had followed the runner, passed third base with him and then backtracked at the merest glimpse of the girl standing alone.

Van Fitzgerald had full advantage over Kate when her eyes ranged back over the field to catch and hold on his. Shocked by the awful coincidence, neither moved a muscle for a long moment, not even to blink, until one of the players tried to reclaim Van's attention.

'Hey, Van,' the other American called in amused tones, 'quit studying the park's natural beauties, boy, and pitch ball.'

The comment was greeted with general laughter that snapped them both out of that first daze. Embarrassed herself, Kate imagined it would make Van Fitzgerald resume the game—only when he scooped up the ball, it was to throw it to his grinning critic with an instruction to take his place. There was more laughter as he began heading towards the lovely dark-haired girl on the edge of their circle.

With all eyes on her, Kate almost broke into a run. Pride overruled the instinct and she turned and walked away. She wouldn't panic. Not this time.

When he drew level, she didn't spare him as much as a glance. Silently he kept up with her, his limp more pronounced as she increased her pace. Another twenty yards and Kate was seething inside—at his persistence, at her own absurd sense of guilt—when he made his move.

A hard hand clamped down on her arm, bringing her to an abrupt halt. 'This is far enough.'

Angrily Kate wheeled around but before she could say a word, she was being dragged to the nearest shade, well out of sight of his friends.

'Take your hands off me!' she hissed when he finally pushed her back against a tree.

'No, I don't think so. This is one conversation that is going to end when *I* feel like it.' He painfully reaffirmed his hold and waited tight-lipped until she gave up struggling. 'Now—why didn't you tell me?'

Kate recognised the same angry question from the previous evening but assumed it had a new meaning. Howard must have revealed she was only his secretary and he was mad because she hadn't.

'It's not my fault you made a fool of yourself,' she snapped, head tilting at an arrogant angle, 'but if you intend to apologise for your behaviour, Mr Fitzgerald, I guarantee you'll have the last word—this time.'

'*Me* apologise?' His brows shot up at the suggestion. 'You have to be kidding!'

'No, merely forgetting you're no gentleman,' she retorted haughtily, and earned herself an even more incredulous stare.

Then on a harsh note he ground out, 'The way I remember it, *lady*, I was the one assaulted just for telling a few home truths. And you'll see me in hell before I take any of it back.'

Kate's eyes narrowed on him. 'Didn't Howard say anything when you went back to the party?'

'Back to the party?' he echoed her words, clearly finding them ridiculous.

'You didn't go back,' she concluded.

'Hardly,' he replied with drawling sarcasm. 'Bayswater may be a classy area but its garbage stinks like anywhere else.'

And the look he shot her told Kate he was referring to more than the rubbish bins into which she'd pushed him. Obviously he hadn't yet seen through Howard's joke. Well, she wasn't about to justify herself.

'I didn't hurt you, did I?' she enquired, but mocking the fact she *had* managed to get the better of him.

His mouth went into an even tighter line. 'I wouldn't push your luck if I were you.'

'Luck? Meeting you again—that's scarcely how I would have termed it,' she continued in the same vein, ignoring the warning in his low undertone. 'Still, they do say bad luck goes in threes.'

'Meaning?' he bit out, daring her to elaborate.

Kate obliged. 'Meaning—I think this hopefully brief encounter makes up my quota, don't you?'

This time Van Fitzgerald didn't even attempt a reply. He just stood rigidly still, staring down at her. How near he was to losing his temper, however, did finally register despite his silence. She tried to walk away, and found herself slammed back against the tree. She made no more sudden moves. His eyes pinned her there, as much a physical force as the hand crushing her shoulder. Eyes no longer laughing, but cold with fury and the desire to hurt.

Thoroughly caught up in the impression of violence emanating from him, Kate actually flinched when he raised his other hand. *Exactly* what he'd intended, she realised—seconds after she felt a light pat on her cheek and saw the satisfied smile registering her show of fear. Furious, she knocked his hand away, but he had only begun humiliating her.

'Such pride,' he murmured as defiance returned to

her eyes. 'Pity there's a price on it. Fifty pounds, wasn't it?'

'Not for you!' Kate spat back.

'No, perhaps not,' he granted far too easily, and at her quick frown, added, 'I had the feeling the sum might be higher for me.'

'That's not what I meant,' she flared back, 'and you know it!'

Her accusation was met with a slight shrug, before he stepped back a pace, and slanting his head, appraised her figure with a slow insolence, infinitely worse than the way he'd looked at her on the balcony last night.

'I agree though,' he said when his eyes finally returned to her face.

'With what?' she demanded, losing track of the conversation.

'Why, that you're worth more, sweet Kate,' he drawled back as if it was the matter under dispute. 'A hundred at least.'

'You—you vile—contemptible . . .' she spluttered in rage.

'I take it that means no,' he cut in, and while she was searching for an adequate response, continued blandly, 'All right, maybe I can improve on the offer.'

'Offer?' Kate was startled into wondering whether he was possibly being serious.

His lips curved. 'Do I detect a note of interest?'

'No, you damn well don't!' she denied hotly, and deciding she'd had enough, more than enough, informed him cuttingly, 'Were I the kind of woman with whom *you* probably *have* to associate, I'd sooner sell myself to the devil. But I'm not, understand?'

If he did, he looked singularly unimpressed. 'You're trying to tell me you're not a hooker.'

'No—I *am* telling you,' she said through clenched teeth.

'Really.' His eyes remained cynical.

'You don't believe me, do you?' she challenged.

He shrugged. 'Does it matter?'

Obviously not to him, and exasperated, Kate gave up. 'Oh, think what you like.'

'Huh-uh—I don't *like*,' he corrected with hard emphasis. 'But I don't intend letting myself be taken for an even bigger fool while you spin me some story. And I won't be making any calls to the Vice Squad, so you can drop the innocent act.'

'Generous of you,' Kate retorted but the sarcasm was wasted on him.

He simply shrugged again. 'I'm not the reforming type. How you mess up your life, honey, is your business.'

'That's not the attitude you took last night,' she said, oddly piqued by his present indifference.

'Yes, well ... I guess I was a little mad when I discovered the way things were between you and Howard,' he admitted, his lips twisting in self-mockery. 'He should have told me from the start. But knowing him, I wouldn't be too surprised if he planned it all as a joke on me.'

Kate almost laughed, suddenly seeing a funny side to the whole affair. The joke was definitely on him, though not in the sense he meant.

'I'm sure he did,' she agreed with such heavy irony it drew a suspicious frown.

'You didn't, by any chance, set it up between you?'

'Set up what?'

'Howard knew I was interested in you and he probably saw me following you out to the balcony. Now, why should he have left us alone if you were supposed to be, let's say, adorning his arm?'

'I'm afraid *I'm* not following *you*, Mr Fitzgerald,' she replied disdainfully, sensing she wouldn't like it when she did.

'Perhaps he was hoping I'd lose my head over you,' he speculated—wildly in Kate's opinion.

'There's an idea,' she muttered drily, thoughts on a nice sharp guillotine slicing down towards his good-looking head.

He might have been reading her mind for his lips quirked into a sudden amused smile. Reminiscent of the man he'd been at the party, it had Kate straightening her own into a tight line. She remembered too well how easy his charm was. She wanted to stay angry.

'Why should he hope that?' she resumed on a scornful note.

He made a face. 'Just Howard's style. As sick jokes go, it would be a beauty. A man falling for a woman, not knowing she was a——'

'You *are* mad!' Kate cut in derisively. 'Stark staring, if you think I'd even *want* you to fall for me. In case you missed the fact, Mr Fitzgerald, I dislike anything that's brash, vulgar or American. You qualify on all three counts.'

'So does Howard,' came the grinning rejoinder as he proved himself impervious to insult.

'That's different!'

'Yes, I appreciate that.'

Kate's forehead creased into a frown. Working out what he might have made of her comment, she decided not to demand an interpretation of his. She stopped believing this was all happening. It wasn't real, she told herself. Then she remembered what was—Johnny waiting for her.

'Since you do, can I go now?' she asked resentfully.

'Why?' he replied.

Kate wondered if he actually imagined she was *enjoying* talking to him. With effort she confined herself to a straight answer.

'I have to meet someone.'

'A John?'

'Yes, but how did . . .' Her voice faded in amazement before she realised just what she'd confirmed—what the phrase *a John* would mean to an American.

'Busy girl,' Van Fitzgerald murmured.

'No, I didn't mean . . . he's my——' she tried to explain.

'Your business,' he dismissed, and not giving a flustered Kate another chance to protest, went on, 'He'll wait. I would . . . for you.'

She didn't believe him. This American wasn't the type of man to do any waiting for a woman. He was simply trying to make her feel more uncomfortable.

'He might come looking for me,' she pursued.

'So?' It was mildly challenging.

'So nothing,' she said in a flat tone. 'Can I go . . . please?'

She pushed away from the tree but he didn't move out of her way.

He did, however, give the matter his consideration before drawling, 'I haven't finished yet.'

'I can't think what else we have to say to each other, Mr Fitzgerald,' she snapped, her patience wearing thin.

'Can't you, sweet Kate?' He made it sound as if she should. Holding her eyes with his, he lost her even more by murmuring, 'I think you might find something to say to a grand . . .'

'A grand what?' she said, frowning.

'A thousand pounds,' he translated.

'What for?' she gasped.

'Don't worry,' he laughed wryly, misreading her mixed look of doubt and horror. 'Nothing fancy. I'm a pretty straight fellow in that respect.'

'You'd give me a thousand pounds just to . . . just to . . .' Kate still refused to accept she'd understood him properly.

'Go to bed with me,' he supplied, ensuring she did.

She stared up at him, searching for signs of madness in the strong lines of his face. She found none. He smiled back, slow and amused, as though he was playing a game with her. He had to be.

'Why are you doing this?' she demanded.

'Maybe I fell after all,' he suggested but his eyes were full of mockery.

'On your head obviously,' she countered sharply, 'if you expect me to be taken in.'

'Taken in?' He raised an eyebrow, all bland innocence. 'You don't believe I have the money,' he surmised, indicating his worn jeans and vest.

Kate glared back at him. 'About as much as I believe you'd pay me a thousand pounds for going to bed with you once.'

'Did I say once? I'm not *that* straight,' he drawled with a wicked smile. 'But I *am* richer than I look.'

Itching to slap his face, Kate retorted rudely, 'Most

people are richer than *you* look, Mr Fitzgerald.'

And felt even more like hitting him when he laughed at her sarcasm. Was he too stupid to recognise he was being insulted?

'It's a wonder you have any clients, sweet Kate, if you treat them all like this. But I wouldn't play too hard to get with me,' he warned almost pleasantly. 'We both know how badly you want the money.'

'I never said——' she began to protest.

'You didn't have to,' he stated, cutting across her. 'I saw how important money was to you last night. Remember?'

When she'd been ready to get down in the gutter for it, he meant. It was his first remark that really hurt. The rest had been ridiculous enough to discount. She said nothing, her face sullen with resentment.

'Why do you need the money?' he asked, and when that also was met with silence, suggested with a surprising hint of compassion, 'To support a kid?'

'No! What do you——' Kate broke off, realising the silliness of asking what he took her for. That was all too obvious.

'A habit then?' he pursued.

'A habit?' she echoed as it conjured up images of black robes and white veils.

'You're either one hell of an innocent or one hell of an actress,' Fitzgerald commented on her puzzled expression. 'Personally I favour the latter.'

'I don't know what you're talking about,' she replied stonily.

'No?' He'd suddenly turned serious again. 'Then show me your arm.'

'What?'

'Show me your arm,' he repeated.

'Why?' Kate demanded, genuinely confused.

'Why not?' he replied, his eyes narrowing on her.

Kate was positively deciding he *was* crazy when he caught her hand, and pushed up the sleeve of her blouse as far as it would go. By the time he did the same with her other arm, examining the fine tracery of veins under her skin, she realised what he was looking for.

'You presumptuous bastard!' she choked out, jerking her arm free.

Visibly shaking with anger, she dragged her sleeves down, and he sighed. 'Okay, it was just a thought. A lot of hookers have drug problems.'

'Not this one!' she hissed back at what was conceivably offered as an apology.

And the moment it was out, thought—'What am I saying?' His craziness was catching. She had to get away from him.

Considering a dash for open ground, she glanced past his shoulder, only to spot her brother sitting on a slope in the distance. Evidently he'd come to find her, and decided not to intrude. Had he misread their apparent intimacy?

Quickly averting her gaze, she garbled out, 'Look, I'm leaving now and if you try to stop me, Mr Fitzgerald, I'll—I'll call for help.'

It was sheer bluff because she'd never risk involving Johnny in this mess. It also had little effect for Fitzgerald simply smiled, confident she wouldn't risk involvement with the police either.

He took a step nearer, closing the gap between them, and she raised her voice to threaten, 'I will!'

'Go ahead,' he invited, his voice softly taunting in contrast.

He was so sure he could treat her any way he liked, he reached for her almost lazily. At Kate's immediate recoil, however, the hands circling her arms tightened to a bruising pressure and she demanded, 'What do you think you're doing?'

'I don't think—I know,' he mocked, already bending his head towards her.

It took Kate only a couple of seconds to react and if her brother's nearness curbed instincts to scratch and slap and kick this time, her rejection was still unmistakable. By twisting her head from side to side, at first she managed to avoid his mouth altogether. But even when a hand left her waist to grip the back of her head, holding it so rigid she could no longer turn her face aside, she did not submit to the kiss. Though his mouth began to grind down on hers, harder, rougher, trying to force an entry past the teeth she kept clenched until her throat was choking with pain, not for a second did she submit.

'Damn you, respond!' he growled in frustration when he eventually raised his head.

'Why the hell should I?' she spat back.

'Respond, and you can go to your John,' was his taut, angry reply.

On the point of refusing outright, Kate hesitated. Any moment her John might come closer towards them—especially if he guessed something was wrong. And what sort of things would the American say to him? Considering some of the possibilities, letting him kiss her seemed the lesser of two evils. But, detesting him as she did, could she fake a response to satisfy his ego? She'd never particularly enjoyed the kisses of some of the young men she *had* liked.

'You promise?' She couldn't mask her distaste but oddly he looked more calculating than angry at it. Calculating what? was the question.

He nodded shortly and while Kate was debating whether to trust him, again lowered his head towards hers. She tensed, expecting him to be brutal, and went even stiffer when his lips barely touched hers. For long seconds that was all he did—brush her mouth with the slow movement of his, but it was the strangest of sensations.

Then a hand came up to caress her neck, the thumb stroking the soft skin of her throat before lightly tilting her head further back. Yet his kiss remained gentle, bewilderingly so, and suddenly from being afraid she would hate what he was forcing on her, she began to fear she wouldn't. She stirred uneasily, desire awakened but unfamiliar to her in the fine trembling of her body. It wasn't to the man, however.

'Put your arms round my neck,' he murmured against her lips.

'I don't think——' she said shakily but the rest was lost as he covered her mouth with his once more.

Later she couldn't explain why she obeyed him. Why

she felt that sharp, sweet ugency to do so—sliding her arms over the damp skin of his bare shoulders and parting her lips for him. A betrayal of weakness which was to be seen in a very different light.

He made some sound, a deep throaty acknowledgement of her surrender, and then his mouth opened hungrily on hers—demanding, giving, destroying resistance as though it had been pretence. Closer and closer he drew her, his hands wandering possessively over her back, almost lifting her when she pressed against the hard length of his body, as near to making love as they could without lying on the green grass. And if the half-savage, half-loving embrace moved far beyond a mere kiss, far from the reluctant response she'd meant to give, it was not Kate who broke away first.

He swore as he abruptly set her back from him and Kate looked at him with startled eyes. Then she understood, catching the grimace of pain on his face as he shifted his weight on to one leg.

'Are you all right?' she asked softly.

'Yes, dammit—it just takes getting used to!' The words were snapped, an impatient rejection of her concern.

It left Kate feeling absurd to have expressed any at all. Nothing had changed. His breathing might be as uneven as her own but, if anything, his eyes were angrier than before. And flushing under his steady stare, already shamed for herself, she didn't have to wonder long what he was thinking of her now.

'As Howard said, you're one class act, baby,' he muttered on a harsh note of insult. 'In fact it's difficult to decide which was the better performance—the put-off or the come-on.'

'I-I didn't——'

'The hell you didn't!' he shouted down her hesitant reply. 'Is that the way you usually do it—have the guy thinking you're a frigid little bitch and then when you go up in flames, the poor sucker gets good and burned?'

'You *made* me,' she said in a choked whisper.

'Did I?' He managed to convey Kate's own doubts in two simple words before dismissing her completely. 'Here—go meet your man.'

She watched, horrified, as he pulled his wallet from a back pocket and counted out some money. He held it out to her.

'I wouldn't take——' she began indignantly.

A humourless laugh cut her short. 'Spare me that routine. I have no intention of paying for the privilege. This is Howard's fifty pounds, that's all. I wouldn't like to have it on my conscience.'

Kate gave him a look that questioned the possibility of him having one. Unaffected, he fanned the notes much as Howard had done last night. Almost as if he knew the temptation it presented.

She wanted to tell him what he could do with his money. Wanted to slap it from his hand. Wanted many things but none as badly as she wanted—*needed*—the fifty pounds. And he knew that too.

He grabbed her hand when she started to back away. 'Here, take it! Call it insurance against any more bad luck!'

Her eyes went from him to the money he'd pressed in her fingers. By some rights, hers—for he'd caused her to drop the original fifty—but it didn't feel that way. More like she really was selling part of herself.

Probably crazy—definitely foolish—but this time when her hand opened it was quite deliberate.

She didn't wait to see if he picked the money off the ground where she let it fall.

CHAPTER FOUR

JOHNNY grinned as she approached. 'Who's that?'

She glanced over her shoulder to find Van Fitzgerald still watching her.

'Nobody.' She turned back and kept walking. 'Come on, or we're going to be late.'

He caught up with her in a couple of strides, wearing an even wider grin.

'Nobody, eh?'

'Yes.'

'Then why were you kissing him?'

'I wasn't.'

'From where I was standing——'

'So you saw,' she snapped at his bantering tone, 'Well, *he* was kissing *me*. There is a difference, you know.'

Whether true or not, it was a stupid thing to say. Kate realised it immediately as Johnny's face fell and he stopped dead in his tracks.

'You didn't want him to, you mean? He was forcing you,' her brother deduced, then in a high voice, demanded, 'Who is he? Do you know him? Or was he——'

'Yes, of course I know him,' she cut in and grabbed Johnny's arm before he could wheel round. 'Listen, he's simply an American I met at Howard's party. I ran into him after you left. And we talked for a while, that's all.'

'He was *kissing* you,' was pointed out—only now as though it was the crime of the century.

'Yes, well ... he sort of fancies me,' she offered lamely, and at her brother's sceptical look, forced a laugh. 'Don't look so amazed. I'm not that repulsive, am I?'

Though he didn't laugh with her, his stance became less aggressive, 'But you don't fancy him?'

'Not much.' Kate's reply was deliberately casual, and with a shrug, she began walking again.

To her relief, Johnny tagged after her, even if he wasn't quite ready to drop the subject. 'Why don't you?' he asked.

Without breaking her step, Kate counted very slowly to ten. Whoever said women were the changeable sex? Undoubtedly a man, she decided, as she considered first Fitzgerald's erratic behaviour and now her brother's. Her own she had already discounted as a moment's insanity, not to be analysed.

'Why should I?' she countered.

Perhaps aware of his inconsistency, Johnny mumbled, 'Dunno. He seemed ... all right.'

Kate mentally raised her eyebrows as words came to

mind. Arrogant, offensive, crude ... an endless list in which the term 'all right' didn't figure at all. She gave Johnny an exasperated glance that silenced him on the matter. And if he returned to it later, it was more obliquely.

'There!' Kate announced with satisfaction as the zip of his second case finally pulled shut. 'You can stop pressing down. Apart from the kitchen sink I think that's everything.'

She hoped so. The two suitcases were bulging at the seams. Most of their contents were of course essential—underwear, shirts, trousers, jerseys—the bulkier clothing for the long winter term. But there were also items best termed miscellaneous—a chess set handmade from plaster of paris, a model Morgan 8, a stack of computer magazines, a half-finished wood carving that just might have been a dog, and a poster of the England rugby team. She'd drawn the line at the dead grass snake.

'Might have been easier with a trunk,' Johnny commented.

'Perhaps,' she agreed, without going into the expense of sending a trunk separately to Suffolk.

'Kate?' he prompted as she redid the careless knot he'd made in his school tie.

'Yes?' she murmured absently.

'Can I ask you something?'

'That sounds ominous. About what?'

'You won't get mad?' he asked.

Which implied she might, but she said, 'I'd sooner hear what's bothering you, Johnny.'

'Well, it's just that you haven't been out with anybody since ... since ages,' he ended vaguely.

Since their parents' death, he meant, and Kate wondered how she should reply. She could hardly say the responsibility of looking after him had left her with little time for relationships over the last two years.

'I haven't met anyone I'm attracted to,' she finally murmured.

'You used to go out with lots of fellows before, Kate,' he pointed out.

'Perhaps, but I seem to recall you weren't that impressed with any at the time.'

'Some of them were okay.'

'Really?' she replied, raising her eyebrows. 'Now what was it you used to call Denis Sackville—the "Dreadful Drip", wasn't it? And as for poor old Willie Partington, you went into paroxysms of laughter every time he said "Oops sorry".'

'Maybe, but you must admit he did say it pretty often,' Johnny stated in his defence. 'Anyway, I was just a kid then. I didn't know any better. I mean if you were to go out with someone now, I'd behave ... impeccably.'

'Impeccably, eh?' she repeated, her lips quirking. He smiled too but his eyes retained a certain earnestness that made her say, 'I'll tell you what, I'll bear it in mind.'

It wasn't a firm promise, more an attempt to stop him worrying about leaving her alone. By the time she deposited him on the Ipswich train, however, he was so bright and breezy she had the feeling he had taken it as such.

And returning to a now oppressively quiet flat, Kate began to wonder if Johnny didn't have a point about her lack of social life. It was certainly lonely while he was away at school. But then she no longer found it easy to make friends. She just wasn't that young girl who used to casually date 'lots of fellows', as Johnny put it, simply to prove her popularity. She was uncertain if she could even act in the same bright careless way now. She'd grown up, and in doing so, acquired sharper, harder edges. She'd had to. Ever since she'd heard of her parents' death ...

They came the morning of the fire, two grim-faced strangers. She fainted when they broke the news to her and came round to find herself half-lying on the living-room couch, with one of the men muttering, 'I didn't expect a girl like her to faint.'

And the other returning more mildly, 'Why not? Whatever else, St Gregory was her father.'

But if there was little sympathy in either of the men's attitudes, it scarcely registered then. She did not even wonder who they were. All she wanted was some privacy in which to give way to grief.

It was debatable whether they would have allowed her that as the one she later knew as Osborne began, 'We need to ask you some questions, Miss St Gregory.'

'Questions?' Her voice was as dazed as her expression, her mind not really with the men at all.

Perhaps the older of the two, Styles, was aware of it because he suggested she lie down for a while before they interviewed her. She managed a nod and had almost forgotten the men by the time she reached her bedroom.

With her face buried in a pillow, she cried for most of the morning, cried until her eyes were swollen and her throat hurting and there were no tears left.

Then the memories came. Images of her dizzy-headed, beautiful mother made sweeter, more poignant by death. And thoughts of her father, thoughts full of regret for the way things had been between them and the lost chance for them ever to be any different.

It was late afternoon before the housekeeper reminded her of the two men downstairs. The storm of weeping had left her feeling detached. She looked it too when she returned to the lounge.

With an effort she recalled the earlier conversation. 'You wanted to ask me something.'

'Yes, that's correct, Miss St Gregory,' Styles confirmed after rising politely at her entrance. 'If we could go somewhere more private, perhaps?'

'As you wish.' Kate led them to her father's study at the end of the hallway and when they were seated, asked, 'Are you from the police?'

'Not exactly. We're Intelligence Officers.' Styles handed her an identity card and watched for her reaction.

Kate gave it a totally puzzled stare, not seeing why her parents' death involved what the card called the Foreign Security division. 'I don't understand. You're investigating the fire?'

'Indirectly,' Styles replied before leaving explanations to Osborne.

'You see the fire was started by an incendiary device, planted in your father's suite. We're interested in who was responsible for it, Miss St Gregory.'

Kate's eyes rounded in shock. 'You're saying someone wanted to kill my father? But that's impossible!' she exclaimed at Osborne's curt nod.

'A man in your father's line of business is bound to be vulnerable to terrorists,' he told her.

'I don't understand,' Kate repeated faintly. 'My father is . . . was a financier——'

'Miss St Gregory, we are well aware what your father's real interests were,' Osborne interrupted brusquely. 'And selling arms to terrorist organisations is a risky business.'

Arms? Kate began to shake her head in stunned disbelief but even as she did, she saw from Osborne's implacable expression, he was telling the truth.

'It's our suspicion one of these groups decided to forgo on payment,' Styles added in his quieter tones.

Still in shock, Kate stared at the men, waiting for them to say more. When they didn't, she gathered they were waiting for *her* to say something. But what?

Impatient with her silence, Osborne resumed, 'I do advise you to co-operate, Miss St Gregory.'

Kate felt the first stirrings of panic as it suddenly struck her that they thought she was feigning ignorance of her father's activities.

'But I don't know anything. How could I?' she appealed, her eyes switching to Styles. Instinctively she sensed he was the more reasonable of the two though he had left much of the talking to Osborne.

And did again as Osborne muttered, 'Come, Miss St Gregory, you expect us to believe that when you've been acting as a courier for your father for the past four months?'

Kate went absolutely white, with a mixture of fear and horror as she realised how her father had used her. The men watched the changing emotions on her face and Styles at least understood.

'You didn't know, did you?' he said on a note of conviction.

Some of the fear receded but the horror remained as Kate choked out, 'What was I carrying?' and when he made no reply, repeated in a voice rising with hysteria, 'On those trips abroad, what was I carrying for him?'

But it was four days later before she was told the part she'd played.

Instead, for hour after hour she relayed every detail she could remember of those trips abroad. Eventually when they'd corrected her several times, she realised they already knew most of it. They were simply testing her willingness to co-operate.

And she was willing. She let them search the house from top to bottom. She even agreed not to disclose her parents' death yet, when they assured her their names would not appear in any newspaper report of the fire.

In the first three days, apart from the servants, the only people she saw were these grim-faced strangers with their endless questions. But if she felt frighteningly alone, she had no desire to confide in anyone. For when the initial shock passed away, she was bitterly ashamed of what her father had been doing to keep them in such lavish style.

On the fourth day, they arrived with a Colonel Lazenby and Kate's imagination ran riot as to why he'd come. Almost beyond fear for herself, her thoughts went to Johnny. As far as she knew, they had no close relations who might look after him if anything happened to her.

And believing this 'Colonel' might be there to arrest her, Kate stared blankly at him when, over morning tea, he politely apologised for any distress caused and thanked her for her co-operation.

At first Kate couldn't believe she'd understood him correctly. 'You're not prosecuting me?'

'For what, Miss St Gregory?' Lazenby said with a supercilious smile. 'We'd look rather silly prosecuting you for your part in things, now wouldn't we?'

Then he went on to explain what she had been delivering for her father. Exactly nothing. Or at any rate, nothing of relevance. It seemed her father was aware of the surveillance he was under. He had merely used her as a decoy, setting up a false trail for others to follow.

'A clever man, your father. I doubt we'll ever be able to establish any real proof of his dealings,' the Colonel admitted.

Kate sighed in relief. At least she wouldn't have to tell Johnny the truth about their father.

'Are your investigations over?' she asked.

'For now, Miss St Gregory,' he returned and his manner suggested they weren't going to forget about her altogether.

But she didn't ask any more questions. She didn't care who had killed her father or why. Each time she thought of him she remembered how he had used her and she felt betrayed.

When they finally departed, Kate drove to Johnny's school. At first he seemed to accept the news almost too well, his face emotionless as they stood facing each other in his housemaster's study. For a moment she felt very remote from the younger brother who spent much of his life away at boarding school. Then the next, he was throwing himself in her arms, no longer the self-contained public schoolboy, but a little boy sobbing his heart out. And she suddenly felt closer to him than she ever had before. She took him home, his half-term holiday only days away anyway, and if the responsibility for him scared her, it gave her strength too. Strength she needed desperately in the coming weeks.

First there were the sympathy calls after she'd inserted a small death notice in the paper. She knew they were well meant but she found them hard to take.

Then there was the visit from Pearson, the family solicitor. She sat rigid with shock while he revealed the house, their home, stood as surety for a massive loan from a finance company, a loan that had to be repaid by the New Year. Evidently the money had been transferred to a Swiss bank account but the lawyer could find no indication of what shares had been secured in return.

Kate could have told him. It had purchased a shipment of arms, lost somewhere en route to Africa.

After that, the bills started to pour in. An endless stream from jewellers and dress shops and catering firms down to the most mundane from local tradesmen. Bills that had mounted up while her father awaited the completion of his latest deal.

Kate tried to settle them all. She sold her parents' cars, then the contents of the house, piece by piece, until she accepted they could not save anything and put what remained up for auction. But the bills kept coming—the most worrying of all a polite request from Johnny's school for the next term's fees, an amount that reflected the famous public school's status.

Finally as Christmas approached, she faced the impossibility of honouring all the debts. She had to think of Johnny, had to look out for his future.

He returned that holiday to find the Hall a great empty house, no longer a home. He stood in the chilly, silent hallway, and looked lost—not so different from the way she felt herself. But he put a brave face on and when Kate explained she had found him a place in a minor public school, he insisted he should leave boarding school altogether so that they could save the fees.

Prepared for such a reaction, Kate had told another lie, an invention about a trust fund their parents had set up for his education. The trust fund—money made from the sale of her own expensive wardrobe and small sportscar—would cover at least the first year of fees at the new school.

But she told him the truth about the debts they would never be able to meet so he would understand the necessity to be discreet about who his parents had been and the precaution of dropping the distinctive 'St' from their surname. And two days after she saw him settled in his new school, she abandoned the house to the finance company.

For almost six months she was running scared, moving from cheap hotels to cheaper hostels as the little money she'd managed to keep back, quickly dwindled.

It took only a matter of days to discover how ill-equipped she was to earn a living. Educated in a private girls' school best described as 'artsy', she had few practical skills to impress an Employment Exchange.

So she accepted the first job offered—as a waitress in a hamburger restaurant—and in between shifts, invested her wages in crash courses in shorthand and typing.

It was a lonely time for Kate, frightened to make friends of the girls at the restaurant or secretarial college in case she was asked any awkward questions.

A hard time too, adjusting to being on her own, learning to think for herself, and, worst of all, constantly living with the fear of being hounded down to pay her father's debts or to face further investigation by the Intelligence Services.

But gradually she began to wonder if anyone was even looking for Katerina St Gregory, to feel safe as plain Kate Gregory, just another young girl of the thousands who flock to London every year.

In the autumn of that first year the future had brightened when she'd landed a secretarial post within days of finishing her course.

She supposed she'd always known her appearance was the reason Howard had picked her above a line of more experienced secretaries, but by then she'd felt tough enough to handle him. And when any disagreement over the tax matter might have threatened her job, she'd decided Johnny's education was her first priority.

And still was, Kate thought, as she lay in bed that night, worrying over how quickly she could find a job. Time enough to make a life for herself when his education was finished; time enough to learn how to trust someone again—without being on her guard, looking for hidden motives, expecting to be used. Anyway, if the events of the last two days were any indication, trustful was probably not the smartest thing to be.

Monday morning Kate made the rounds of the secretarial job agencies in the West End. Dressed in a smartly tailored skirt suit and with her hair coiled in a becoming chignon, she was at least confident of her appearance. But very quickly she came to realise how lucky she had been to get that post with Howard. It seemed that if she could type and take shorthand at a reasonable rate, she was severely lacking in other directions. Apart from being too young for the better business posts, she'd never been within a mile of a word processor, knew only the basics of filing and had no commercial experience whatsoever.

And when she eventually found a bureau specialising in social secretary work, she discovered her problems were just beginning, although at first the interviewer had been enthusiastic.

'*The* Howard Carson,' the woman repeated, clearly impressed.

Sincerely hoping there wasn't more than one Howard Carson, Kate confirmed, 'Yes, the author.'

'I've read all his books—marvellous writer,' the woman continued extravagantly. 'Tell me, what's he like to work for?'

Impossible, tyrannical, boorish Kate thought. But she could hardly say so. The interviewer was obviously an admirer.

'Very nice,' she replied, crossing her fingers. 'I'm only sorry he decided to return to America.'

'Well, never mind, dear,' she was offered a friendly smile, 'I'm sure we'll be able to find you something suitable.'

'How soon?' Kate hoped she didn't sound too desperate.

'Oh, quite quickly I should imagine. After we've taken up your references of course ... Is there something wrong?'

'No, I ...' Kate thought rapidly. 'It's just that Mr Carson might be difficult to contact. He travels so much.'

'Mm, I quite understand. These jet-setters.' The interviewer flashed her another smile. 'In that case, perhaps we could accept a testimonial until we receive a reference.'

'A testimonial?' Kate echoed, earning her first frown.

'Yes, I assume Mr Carson provided one before he left.'

'Well, actually . . . no.'

'No? But if he can't be contacted, how do you expect us to evaluate your capabilities?'

'I didn't think. I mean I forgot to ask him. He was very busy the last few days and . . .' Kate babbled on while the woman's look grew more and more sceptical, her questions terser until finally the interview was concluded with a few abrupt words.

After that she sat in a coffee house, screwing up courage to make a phone call and working out what she should say. It wasn't easy. She had never felt less like being tactful. What could she say? 'I'm sorry I ran out on your party, Howard. Don't worry about your little joke. Loved it when I saw the point.'

Like hell, she muttered to herself, positive the words would stick in her throat. But what other choice did she have? Howard was leaving for America on Wednesday.

In the end she decided to hope for on-the-spot inspiration, only to find herself talking to a recording machine. After a couple of false starts she managed, 'This is Kate. Could you provide me with a reference . . . please?'

When she hung up, she instantly regretted making it so bare. Undoubtedly her 'please' had sounded as forced as it was.

Clearly she wasn't going to get a permanent job without that reference. She had to hope Howard had a conscience, although she had little evidence to support the idea. Deciding any job was better than none, she went to a 'temping' agency. There, she discovered an even greater problem.

They weren't so particular about a reference after they tested her shorthand and typing speeds. It was Kate herself who went through several shades of colour before settling on a panicked white when they announced they'd write to her tax office for a replacement to her 'lost' tax certificate.

Another interview was hastily concluded, this time by a stammering Kate.

She walked around aimlessly for an hour before trailing home. There didn't seem anything else she could do. She hadn't the money to pay the tax she must owe. Even if she had, any attempt to do so might put Howard in an awkward position. And what sort of reference would he give her then?

While she was trying—and failing miserably—to find a way out of the situation, there was a knock at the door. She stared blankly at the pretty blonde on the other side.

'Hello, I'm the new tenant on the first floor. Are you Kate?'

'Yes.'

'Telephone. An American, I think,' the girl smiled. 'He phoned a couple of times earlier but you were out.'

'Thank God,' Kate thought. With Howard returning her call so promptly, it might mean her luck was changing.

'Thanks, er——?'

'Sally.'

'Thanks, Sally,' she called over her shoulder as she raced up to the telephone on the first-floor landing.

'Howard,' she gasped into the receiver and waited for him to speak. When he didn't she repeated more anxiously, 'Howard?'

'I'm afraid not,' murmured a wry voice that seemed familiar even before it went on hesitantly, 'It's Van ... Van Fitzgerald. Howard's just put me straight. And well, Kate, what can I say?'

Stunned for a moment, Kate herself said nothing. Then recovering, she made it resoundingly clear that was exactly how much she wanted to hear him say by slamming the phone back on its hook.

'Short call,' Sally commented as they passed on the stairs.

'Yes,' Kate replied, colouring slightly, and carried on down to her flat. The telephone went again as she reached her door.

'Kate?' Sally yelled and when she reappeared halfway up the stairs, shouted down, 'The same bloke I think.'

'Oh, could you possibly . . .'

'Tell him you're out?' Sally astutely suggested.

Kate gave her a grateful smile. 'If you wouldn't mind.'

Plainly enjoying herself, Sally uncovered the mouth-piece and said, 'Sorry, she's gone out . . . Yes, it was sudden. I believe she just received some bad news over the 'phone.'

Kate shared the other's grin at this embellishment and decided she liked her new neighbour.

'Okay, I'll pass on a message . . . Tell her—tell her *what*?' The blonde girl's brows rose. 'Now? But she's . . . all right, hold on . . .'

Sally put her hand on the mouthpiece and, leaning over the wooden banister, said to Kate, 'I think your caller's crazy.'

'He is!'

'Anyway, he wants you to know he's in hell. Says you'll understand——'

Kate didn't for a second or two. Then she recalled him angrily swearing she'd see him in hell before he apologised.

'—And if you don't come to the phone, he'll come and humble himself in person,' Sally continued to relay faithfully.

'No!' Kate almost shrieked as she flew back up the remaining stairs. Fitzgerald at the far end of a telephone was bad enough. She gave Sally an apologetic look for involving her but the other girl grinned broadly before disappearing into her flat.

Then she snapped into the phone, 'Yes?'

'Kate?'

'Yes,' she repeated even more coldly at the tentative opener.

'You can't imagine how bad I feel, Kate,' Fitzgerald continued in a subdued tone, the nearest he could probably get to humility. 'After the way I treated you yesterday . . . well, you must think me a first-class louse.'

There was a long pause Kate assumed she was meant to fill. She resisted the temptation.

Eventually he came back, 'Speak to me, Kate. If it's only to agree.'

'All right, I agree—you're a first-class louse,' Kate said stonily, refusing to be charmed. 'Was there anything else, Mr Fitzgerald?'

'Kate ... listen, this is impossible over the 'phone. Let me come and see you.'

'No!'

'What's your address?' he pursued. 'Or we could meet in a pub if you want.'

'No, I—my address?' Kate picked up on the question that had struck a wrong note. 'You haven't got it?'

'Damn,' came softly over the line as he realised his mistake. 'No, Howard wouldn't give it to me. But if you hang up, Kate, I'll keep ringing. I swear it.'

'Be my guest,' she muttered before once more cutting him off.

True to his word, the phone rang immediately. She stood staring at it, not sure what to do. All four floors shared the same number so she could hardly leave it off the hook. But the last thing she wanted was to listen to any more of his persuasive drawl.

She was still debating the problem when Sally reappeared in her doorway. Kate gave an embarrassed smile, feeling silly standing guard over the ringing telephone.

Sally, however, seemed to understand, commenting, 'Persistent type, isn't he?'

'Among other things,' Kate agreed drily. 'I'm sorry if it's annoying.'

'Don't worry about it. Look, why don't you come in for a cuppa and we'll see how long he keeps ringing?' The other girl grinned, and led the way into the flat.

Despite their difference in background, the two women were soon chatting easily. Over coffee, Sally gave her a potted biography that amounted to the fact she'd been brought up in Yorkshire, didn't fancy marrying the boy next door and had come to London to make her fame and fortune as a model.

'Is it difficult to get into fashion modelling?' Kate

asked, thinking it must be for Sally definitely had the looks and figure to be successful.

'Murder,' Sally groaned. 'My portfolio's not bad, but my accent tends to put them off.'

'I wouldn't have thought that mattered.'

'Seems to. Times have changed since Twiggy. More of your deb types go in for it. In fact, bet you'd do all right,' Sally stated generously as she assessed Kate's dark, fine-boned looks. 'You've got class.'

Kate's smile was more wry than anything. It was the third time in so many days this had been said of her. She was beginning to consider it a very doubtful compliment. It certainly had been in Fitzgerald's case.

'Hey, it's stopped,' Sally announced as the telephone gave one last, long ring and then silence. 'Twenty minutes—he must be keen.'

'Not really. I don't think he'll call again,' Kate replied—wishful thinking. 'But if he does . . .'

'You've emigrated?' the blonde girl supplied with a conspiratorial grin. 'What's he done, this American?'

'It's a long story,' Kate sighed.

'Well, if you need an ear,' Sally offered.

There was no pressure to confide which was perhaps why she did. Not all of it of course, but enough for Sally to understand her unwillingness to take his calls.

'A thousand pounds just to . . .' Her eyes widened expressively. 'He must be bonkers about you.'

'I'd stop at bonkers,' Kate muttered half-seriously. 'And he had no intention of actually paying me. He made that quite clear at the end.'

'But only after it became obvious you weren't interested,' Sally pointed out.

Had it been like that? Kate's thoughts drifted back to the scene in the park. This time as an observer, watching two figures straining together for more than a kiss under the shadow of the trees. A moment's madness on her part. But how uninterested had she seemed then? And his rejection had been immediate.

'He's not the sort of man to pay for the privilege,' she quoted Fitzgerald himself.

'You'd be surprised,' Sally stated with a worldly-wise

air. 'After all, you haven't made him sound the answer to a maiden's prayer. More your standard, loud-mouthed creep. If he's that unattractive——'

'He isn't!' Kate interrupted without thinking, and instantly wished she hadn't. Sally was waiting for her to explain her emphatic denial and for no good reason she blushed. 'I mean he's a creep, like you said, but he also happens to be a good-looking one.'

'Oh,' Sally murmured, investing a great deal of meaning into the single syllable. 'Funny, you didn't mention that before.'

'Didn't I?' Kate parried with an innocent air that made the other laugh.

'How good-looking?' she asked.

Kate's mind pictured amused blue eyes, creased at the corners, and strangely, despite events, that flashing smile he had. Reluctant to attempt a description, she answered with a shrug she hoped would convey indifference. Perhaps it did for Sally changed the subject.

'I think I met your brother last week. Helped me carry my junk up. He seems a nice kid.'

'Most of the time.' Kate smiled fondly. 'He was quite taken himself, I believe. He said the new tenant was a dishy blonde.'

'Thanks for telling me,' Sally grinned. 'Makes a change to get a decent compliment. Mostly the suggestive variety I get at the club.'

'The club?'

'Genevieve's, up along the Bayswater,' Sally explained after a moment's hesitation—sometimes people ceased being friendly when they knew how she supplemented her modelling. 'I work there weekends. Not too bad if you're on the games tables and it's good money—straight cash too.'

Kate's ears picked up. She wondered if she'd understood correctly.

'Straight cash, you mean . . .?'

'No tax. Officially we don't earn enough. Customers leave tips and that's where the real money is.' She saw Kate's face form a very serious frown. 'You're shocked?'

'No.' Kate was tempted to admit she had no right to be. 'In fact, how would you go about getting a job like that?'

'Through friends usually.' Sally leaned forward to stub out her cigarette and read more than passing interest in Kate's expression. 'You're not talking about yourself, are you?'

'Why not? I have been in a casino, you know,' Kate said, realising she might appear naïve to the more experienced girl.

She did. Despite her current circumstances, everything about Kate implied a sheltered, moneyed background to an astute Sally.

'At Monte Carlo by any chance?' the blonde girl asked and at Kate's surprised nod, laughed. 'Oh, love, the Genevieve might as well be on a different planet for all they have in common. If I were you, I'd concentrate on getting your ex-boss to come up with a reference.'

'I suppose you're right,' Kate sighed.

'I am,' Sally claimed with a grin. 'And who knows—maybe he's sorry too?'

'Maybe,' Kate agreed, but not holding out much hope.

Right at that moment she would have considered Howard the lowest form of life if the position wasn't already filled.

CHAPTER FIVE

IN fact Kate's opinion of one of the Americans was to undergo a change the very next day, when mid-morning Sally once more appeared at the door to announce she was wanted on the telephone, this time by a Howard.

'That's my old boss,' Kate said with a slight grimace. 'Thanks for coming down to tell me.'

'No bother. I was on my way out.' Sally indicated her raincoat and departed with the advice, 'Go give him hell, love.'

Kate only wished she could. Instead she said tentatively, 'Is that you, Howard?'

'Yeah, Kate,' was sighed heavily over the line and then silence.

'Did you get my call about a reference, Howard?' she prompted.

'Sure did, Kate.' He took the cue gratefully. 'And don't worry. After what I did, you deserve the best.'

Was this Howard talking? Kate wondered if she was having delusions.

'All I can say, is that I was pretty drunk,' he continued in the same apologetic tone. 'Not much of an excuse, I realise. Van's made that clear.'

'He called me.'

'Yes, I know. He says you keep slamming the phone down on him.'

'Howard, you won't give him my address, will you?'

'Not if you don't want me to ... but, Kate, why won't you see him? He just wants to make his apologies.'

'He already has,' she said on an uncompromising note.

'Yes, but he says ... he says you wouldn't accept them,' Howard replied after a pause. Its significance was not lost on Kate.

'Howard, is he there with you now?' she challenged.

'No, er ... what makes you think that?'

'Woman's intuition,' Kate said drily although it was more the obvious way in which he was lying. 'Well, Howard, if you were to see Mr Fitzgerald sometime, perhaps you could tell him for me that he can take his apologies and stick——'

'Okay, Kate. I've got the general idea,' Howard interrupted with a nervous laugh. 'It really was my fault though.'

'He didn't *have* to believe you, did he?' Kate pointed out, convinced she was talking to more than Howard.

'No, but——' Howard hesitated, perhaps for consultation. 'There are reasons he did. Difficult to explain over the phone, but if we could meet for lunch?'

Kate smelled a rat—a big blond Irish-American one.

'I don't think so.'

'Please, Kate.' He was almost begging. Not Howard's
style at all. And oddly, she found it easier to be
forgiving with him.

'All right, but Howard . . .'

'Yes?'

'You will be alone?'

'I give you my word,' he said without needing an
explanation, and arranged a time and place before
ringing off.

Kate changed into more formal dress. They were
lunching at the Belvedere, the restaurant in the grounds
of Holland Park. It was so near to her flat she could
walk there. While she did, she ran over in her mind the
things she intended to say. Perhaps his generous mood
would disappear if she brought up the tax matter, but
she had to try.

She arrived at the stroke of twelve to find Howard
already waiting at a table, but any rehearsed speech
went clean out of her head the moment she saw his
face.

'Wh-what happened?' she gasped, staring in horror at
the bruising on his jaw and below one eye, not quite
concealed by dark glasses.

'You should see the other fellow.' He smiled, then
winced at the effort it cost.

'Fitzgerald,' she murmured sickly as she sank into a
chair.

'And not a mark on him,' Howard admitted with a
short laugh. 'Whoever coined the phrase "the fighting
Irish" knew what they were talking about.'

'But why?' she asked, shaking her head in disbelief.

'I guess he doesn't like my sense of humour.'

Neither did Kate, but this . . .

'He came to see me yesterday for your phone
number,' Howard went on at her shocked silence. 'By
that time I was feeling kinda ashamed myself. I'd tried
to get you a couple of times on Sunday. When I realised
Van still had the wrong idea about you, I decided I'd
better tell him the truth.'

'And he hit you,' Kate filled in for herself.

'Like a sledgehammer,' Howard confirmed with an almost humorous groan.

But Kate didn't share his amusement. 'He asked you for my telephone number *before* you told him I was really your secretary?'

Howard nodded and reading her deepening scowl, rushed on, 'Listen, I know how it looks, Kate, but believe me, that just isn't Van's style. Me, yes—when we were in the army together in Vietnam, I used to pick up the occasional bar girl. A lot of the guys did. But Van, no. He didn't seem to want that kind of sex.'

'Then why did he want my number?' Kate wasn't convinced.

'I'm not sure,' Howard murmured thoughtfully, 'but in my opinion, it was *despite* what he imagined you were. In fact—he'll probably kill me for telling you this, Kate—but I have a notion the guy has it bad for you.'

Kate nearly laughed aloud at this absurd speculation, wondering how Fitzgerald acted towards girls he *didn't* like if his behaviour to her was mistaken for infatuation.

'Well, Howard, whatever the *it* he's got,' she muttered cynically, 'I trust it proves fatal.'

'Aw, Kate, you don't mean that,' he reproved, to be given a hard glance that said she did. 'Take it from me, honey, he's a man worth knowing.'

Kate gazed incredulously at the bruised and battered face opposite her. 'Howard, I seem to remember the day after I met your friend, you warned me to avoid him like the plague.'

'Yeah, perhaps I did. But goddammit, Kate, you must have realised why by now,' he drawled back, sounding more the usual Howard, and at her puzzled look, added bluntly, 'I was interested in you myself, and getting nowhere fast. With Van on the scene, even I know I don't stand much of a chance. He may not be the playboy I made out, but women sure as hell seem to like him.'

'*Some* women, Howard,' she stressed, excluding herself from that number. 'And I really don't understand why you're defending him now, especially after he's beaten you up.'

'A couple of punches isn't exactly beating up, Kate,' he pointed out with a wry smile. 'He could have hurt me worse than this if he'd had a mind to. But he's usually a pretty good-natured guy and I'd like to set things right between the two of you. So if you could meet him, Kate honey—for a drink or something?'

Kate frowned. Perhaps she could now see why Fitzgerald had been ready to believe Howard's insinuations about her, but every instinct warned her to keep away from the man.

'No, I'm sorry, Howard, just tell him to forget the whole thing.'

'Come on, Kate, don't be so hard on him,' Howard coaxed, as though she was somehow in the wrong. But it only made her adamant.

'No, Howard, and if you're here simply to act as a go-between for him, I'd sooner forget lunch too.'

'Okay—listen, I won't mention his name again,' he inserted quickly as she made to pick up her bag. 'Look, why don't we order?'

She subsided back in her chair and accepted the menu pressed on her. Surprisingly he kept his word throughout the meal, and even more surprisingly, his company was as pleasant as their surroundings.

'Have you started looking for another job?' he asked when the first course was served.

'Yes, that's why I need a reference.'

'I have it with me.' He drew an envelope out of his inside pocket and she tucked it away in her handbag.

'I might need you to confirm it separately,' Kate went on, working her way towards mentioning the other obstacle.

'That's fine. My New York address is inside. You've something lined up?'

'No, nothing definite.'

Howard seemed to hesitate before saying, 'In that case, I have a friend who needs a secretary. But perhaps you wouldn't be interested.'

'A writer?'

'Yes—American too.' He watched as Kate's face lost some of its initial enthusiasm, and smiled ruefully. 'I guessed you might not wish to repeat the experience.'

'No, it's not that,' she denied. 'It's just ... what if your friend asks for my P45?'

'Your what?' Howard raised his eyebrows.

'It's a tax certificate,' she explained, treading carefully. 'You have to hand it over to a new employer, only mine's out of date. And if he sends it to the tax office, they might wonder why.'

'Oh, I see. No problem,' he dismissed so casually Kate could have struck him before he added, 'I'll get my accountant to square your back dues.'

'You will?' She couldn't believe it was going to be that easy.

He nodded. 'Don't worry, I'll take care of it.'

'Thanks, Howard,' she said with enormous relief.

'Don't thank me, Kate. I shouldn't have suggested any monkey business with your taxes in the first place.'

She made no reply to that, considering how little persuasion she'd needed. Instead she pursued, 'About that job, what would it entail?'

'Roughly the same as you did for me. Less on the social side probably. But maybe you'd prefer a complete change, so don't feel I'm trying to talk you into it.'

She didn't—quite the opposite it seemed. 'You sound as though you don't think it would be a good idea.'

Again he hesitated. 'I'm not sure you'll like ... Pete—Peter Holstein, that's his name, by the way. He's pretty different from me.'

Kate smiled inwardly but confined herself to saying, 'To be honest, Howard, I need to find a job as quickly as possible. I only hope your friend likes me.'

'Oh, he'll like you, all right,' Howard told her with a wry smile. 'Of that, I *am* sure.'

And if Kate was slightly uneasy at something in Howard's manner, the feeling passed long before lunch was over. They parted on almost friendly terms. She went home, her spirits higher than they had been for days. Howard seemed positive that, with his recommendation, an interview would be a mere formality.

Indeed, a letter arrived from this Peter Holstein two days later, suggesting a meeting on Monday morning at nine. She wrote back, confirming the appointment. Of course she worried whether she would like him or not. She knew no more than the fact that he was a writer—war stories of all things—but for a good salary she thought she could put up with almost anyone. After all, Howard at his worst hadn't been the easiest of employers.

But her confidence faded over the weekend, while her worries increased on calculating and re-calculating her finances. She hadn't saved a penny yet towards Johnny's fees for the spring term and she already owed the landlady a few weeks' rent. She badly needed a job, and if Howard's friend took a dislike to her, it might be some weeks before her tax situation was straightened out sufficiently for her to apply elsewhere. So the interview with Peter Holstein began to appear frighteningly important.

By Monday morning it had reached nightmare proportions. Her nerves were ragged; on less than five hours' sleep, her face was drawn with an unhealthy pallor; and yawning—she couldn't seem to stop.

In fact her mouth was stretched wide just as the doorbell was answered. For a first impression, it was not the best. Luckily, she also seemed to have come to the wrong flat.

'Yes?' A large figure filled the doorway, dressed in flowered apron and headscarf.

Kate frowned. The address on the American's letter had turned out to be an old Georgian mansion in South Kensington, converted into service flats. The porter had directed her up to the third floor—but had he said right or left out of the lift?

'I'm looking for a Peter Holstein who lives on this floor.'

'Holstein?' The woman shook her head from side to side. 'Not on this floor, dear.'

'But——' Kate checked her letter—definitely third as the porter confirmed. 'Are you certain? He's a writer.'

'Oh, Lord love us, it's himself you'll be meaning!' The

woman's face broke into a wide, friendly smile. 'And sure I'll be forgetting my own name next. But it's his whatsit you see.'

'His whatsit?' Kate echoed.

'You know——' The other waved her hand expressively by way of explanation before running on, 'And you'll be the secretary he's mentioned. Come away in with you, then.'

Slightly bemused, Kate followed her down a long narrow hallway to an end room on the right.

'I'm Mrs O'Reilly, his daily,' the woman introduced herself, and then glancing round the room, confided, 'Although if you ask me, I'd say it would be more an *hourly* he'd be needing.'

Mrs O'Reilly laughed loudly at her own joke and Kate allowed herself a smile when she saw the point. It would have been a nice room—but for the books, newspapers and overflowing ashtrays scattered everywhere.

'Perhaps you'll be keeping him tidy,' Mrs O'Reilly suggested with another broad smile.

'Perhaps,' Kate agreed, although she didn't hold out much hope. To create as much chaos over what she assumed was a weekend, its inhabitant must have had a lifetime of practice. 'Actually, I haven't met him yet. This is only an interview I've come for,' she added.

'Oh well, it's a treat you have in store,' Mrs O'Reilly chuckled. 'He's a lovely man despite his clutter. One of us at heart, you know.'

'Us?'

'The Irish, dearie.'

'Oh yes,' Kate murmured but feeling she could be excused her slowness. The name Holstein hardly conjured up visions of the Emerald Isle, even a few generations removed.

While Mrs O'Reilly disappeared to fetch the *lovely man*, Kate stood nervously in the middle of the room, wondering what to expect of its owner.

The furniture was large and old-fashioned—a velvet smoking-chair, leather sofa, lead-paned bookcases crammed full, a walnut bureau—odds and ends that made an attractive whole. A room to be lived in, comfortable rather than luxurious. She was forming a pleasant image of a grey-haired academic when Mrs O'Reilly returned.

'He'll be with you in a tic. I'm afraid I was late this morning so he slept in.'

Kate, recalling her effort to be here on the dot of nine, wished she could have had the same privilege. But she smiled politely at the confidence.

'He's a grand sleeper,' the Irish woman continued, obviously regarding it as an enviable quality. 'Never hears an alarm. Of course he'd have to be like that, what with the bombs and all.'

Now totally at a loss, Kate smiled even more politely. The *bombs*? she repeated to herself, wishing Howard had been more expansive on the subject of Peter Holstein. Either the man had a strange taste in cleaning women or she herself was missing some essential details required to follow the conversation.

'I suppose so,' she eventually offered.

'Still, it's to be hoped he'll be settling for a little peace now,' the Irish woman said with a heavy sigh. 'High time a man of his age settled down altogether, to my mind.'

'How old is he?' Kate murmured, at least understanding the last remark to mean Holstein was unmarried.

'Thirty-seven and never once been within kneeling distance of the altar,' Mrs O'Reilly confirmed in her colourful way, then shaking her head over it, added, 'But I'd better not be saying more. He's told me I mustn't scare you off before he has a chance to talk to you. Though why he imagines I'd do that, I don't know.'

At this Kate had to hide a smile. Presumably Holstein was aware of the disconcerting effect Mrs O'Reilly might have.

'Anyway, I'll be getting back to the kitchen,' she resumed cheerily. 'Would you like tea or coffee, dearie?'

'Whichever's easier,' Kate replied.

'Mr Van always has coffee,' she was informed.

'In that case, I'll have——' she stopped mid-sentence as her mind backtracked violently. 'Mr who——?'

'Oh, that's what I call him. Doesn't insist on formalities, does Mr Fitzgerald. But it didn't seem right using only his——'

Kate didn't hear the rest. She was heading for the front door at a run when she collided with the man emerging from one of the bedrooms. Hair ruffled, face unshaven, but all too unmistakably Van Fitzgerald. For a moment they simply stared at one another, then, unbelievably, he offered her a slight smile in greeting, 'Good morning, Kate.'

And Kate exploded. 'You absolute, total, despicable bastard!'

'Now wait a minute, Kate, I'm sorry if——' he began pleasantly enough but was left talking to himself as Kate brushed past him.

She made it to the door but he caught her before she could lift the latch. A firm hand on her arm, he pulled her away and swivelled round to back her against a wall.

Struggling futilely and meaning it this time, she threatened, 'Get your hands off me or I'll start screaming!'

'You already are, Kate,' he pointed out, his quieter tone emphasising the fact.

But he released her arms and took a step backwards. Standing between her and the door, he had her trapped anyway. Accepting it, Kate let her eyes express her feelings, venomous with dislike. He grimaced and ran a hand through his dishevelled hair.

'How about if I allow you a few free punches? Would that make you feel any better?'

'How about if you walk under a bus!' she retorted on a suspiciously serious note.

'Any particular number?' he returned, but the coaxing smile on his lips died when tiredness and anger and disappointment suddenly caught up with Kate in a reaction that was totally involuntary.

For the first tear had fallen before she was even aware of it, and as a second slid down her cheek, she could have echoed Fitzgerald's stunned, 'You're crying . . .'

'What have you been doing to her?' came from Mrs O'Reilly, abandoning her role as impartial observer.

'Nothing.'

'Looks like it.'

'I'll explain later,' he said shortly, all his attention focused on Kate, head now bent intent on blinking back any more tears. 'Why don't you make her a cup of tea, huh?'

'Huh!' Mrs O'Reilly echoed with a snort as she took herself off to the kitchen.

Van placed a comforting hand on Kate's shoulder but it was angrily shrugged off. Through stifled sobs he distinguished, 'I don't want your bloody tea.'

And Kate heard him sigh with what she assumed was exasperation before he drawled, 'You could always look on it as Mrs O's bloody tea.'

'Stop making fun of me!' she managed to snap, dashing away her shameful tears with the back of her hand.

'Then stop making me feel like something you found under a stone,' he rapped back, losing patience. 'I've said sorry. What more do you want?'

Kate stared up at him. Did he really believe she was crying over his earlier behaviour? It was nothing compared with his latest—getting Howard to entice her here, tricking her into thinking she had the chance of a job, and, perhaps worst of all, making her feel she had been very foolish not to see through the whole scheme.

'Come on.' This time he didn't let her pull away. 'Let's at least discuss it.'

Kate couldn't see anything to discuss but her legs felt shaky as he guided her back to the lounge and she sank almost willingly into a chair. She took a handkerchief out of her bag and dried her eyes.

Fitzgerald sat watching her from the settee opposite and after a lengthy silence murmured, 'You don't look too good.'

'Thanks,' she said caustically, discounting the concern in his voice.

'No, I mean it,' he stressed.

Was that intended to make her feel better? Kate wondered, glaring at him.

'What have you been doing to yourself?' he pursued.

'Use your imagination! You're good at that, remember?' Kate was snapping back just as Mrs O'Reilly entered with a tray of tea and toast.

'You two know each other, I take it,' said the older woman, glancing from one taut expression to another.

'As you can hear,' Fitzgerald replied, mocking Kate's ready temper, but when the Irish woman lingered, making it plain she'd decided a chaperon was required, he added, 'Why don't you go dust up a storm in one of the bedrooms, Mrs O? Kate'll scream again if she wants you.'

At this Mrs O'Reilly drew up her large bosom in a huff of disapproval, slid him a look that would have soured milk, and then on a contrasting note of kindness, said to Kate, 'You do that, dear, if you feel the need.'

When she withdrew with a last stern glance in Fitzgerald's direction, he remarked, 'I get the impression I'm not her blue-eyed boy any more.'

'I didn't tell her anything!' Kate denied.

'No, I assume you were in full flight the second she let my name drop.'

'Which one?' she retorted bitterly. 'The porter downstairs seems to know you by your alias.'

'I think you mean pseudonym,' he corrected, tone wry.

His 'whatsit' Kate realised, but she muttered back, 'Do I?'

'Okay, so I acted a little shadily,' he conceded. 'But I do write under the name Holstein.'

'Really.'

'And if you're interested——'

'I'm not!'

'—I *am* in the market for a good secretary,' he finished, ignoring her interruption.

Kate's response was incredulous. 'You think I'd work for you!'

'You could do worse. After all, you worked for

Howard,' he said on an amused note, and observing her spark of anger at the name, added, 'He sends his apologies, by the way.'

'You forced him to—to set me up, didn't you?' she accused.

'Let's say persuaded.' He shrugged.

Kate wasn't impressed by the euphemism. 'I've seen your methods of persuasion.'

'He deserved it,' he returned curtly and dismissing the subject altogether, rose to pour the tea. 'Milk?'

Kate gave a brief nod rather than argue she still did not want his tea.

'Sugar?' he enquired, smiling.

'No ... thank you,' she ground out, aware of how absurd social niceties could be on occasion.

He placed her cup on a small table beside her chair.

'Toast?'

She shook her head, too wound up to stomach food.

Fitzgerald obviously didn't have the same problem. He sat down and polished off several slices before resuming the conversation.

'Well, what do you think?' he suddenly asked while Kate was contemplating her next move—considering whether she could catch him off-guard with another bolt for the front door.

'Of what?' she replied blankly.

'Being my secretary,' he supplied patiently.

'Your *secretary*—you can't be serious!'

'Why not?'

Kate stared back at him, unable to find a rational reply. He was exasperating, unscrupulous and right this second, she could hardly bear to be in the same room with him—but besides all that—why not?

'I'd expect you to do some research, decipher my notes and type my manuscript,' he continued at her silence.

'That's all?' she blurted out.

'What else?' It was said with a shrug but there was a definite smile lurking in his eyes as they met hers head on.

It brought back the incident in the park, and a scarlet

flush to Kate's fine cheekbones. His smile became mocking, as though he could read every thought in her head. And perhaps he could because it disappeared the moment she made the smallest move to rise.

'That's *all*,' he stressed quickly. 'And if you're still bothered as to why I wanted your number last week, it was to give you another chance to collect that fifty once you'd cooled down. Okay?'

'Yes.' Kate nodded. It made sense, better sense than any other explanation possible.

'Listen, I do need a secretary and, according to Howard, you're as efficient as any I'd find through an agency. I'll pay you three grand more than he did—before tax, of course. That way you should come out with the same so you don't have to worry.'

Did he have to put it like that? Kate fumed. As well as drawing attention to her dishonesty, he seemed to be reminding her of the desperation she'd shown over money.

'I wasn't,' she said coldly.

'Good. Any questions?'

'What happened to your last secretary?' she asked in a tone that couldn't be taken as anything but insultingly suspicious.

'She was useless,' he drawled back, face straight, 'so I sold her to white slavers.'

'White sla—very funny!' Kate snapped at him.

'Sorry,' he grinned unrepentantly, 'but I had the feeling you expected something suitably dire. Actually, you'll be the first. The same goes for the book.'

Kate frowned. 'I thought you already did war stories,' she said and that seemed to amuse him too, making her wonder if it was another of Howard's fabrications. Perhaps everything had been.

'Up until this summer, I was a correspondent,' he told her.

'A correspondent? You mean you wrote——' Kate trailed off as Mrs O'Reilly's earlier remarks made an incredible sense.

'War stories,' he echoed her description but with a sardonic smile that knew perfectly well she'd been thinking of the boys' comic variety. Then on a more serious vein, he went on, 'To a certain extent, the book is one too. You're not squeamish, are you?'

'No, I don't think so but——'

'Good. Can you start tomorrow?'

'Well, I——'

'Fine. You're hired.'

'But——'

CHAPTER SIX

'BUT you took the job?' Sally asked after listening to a rather confused account of Kate's morning.

'I don't know.' Kate was still trying to work that out for herself. 'I don't even remember him giving me the chance to say yes or no, and the next moment he was formally introducing me as his secretary to Mrs O'Reilly, the daily.'

'You must have said something,' Sally insisted.

Kate shook her head with the same helplessness that she'd felt earlier. 'I think I was in shock. I mean him—a war correspondent! It just seemed too ridiculous for words.'

'I don't know. He has enough nerve for it at any rate,' Sally pointed out.

'Oh, he has that!' Kate agreed, her eyes flashing angrily. 'But correspondents are the sort of journalists you imagine to have ideals, some sense of integrity. I doubt if Fitzgerald has ever had a serious thought in his life, far less a high regard for the truth.'

'Maybe he's different underneath,' Sally suggested. 'After all, he might have tricked you but it was with good intentions.'

'It was?' Kate couldn't quite see them.

'Sure—offering you a job, I mean. That was nice, wasn't it?' Sally reasoned.

'Was it?' Kate's expression was now totally sceptical.

'Well, he could get a really good secretary for that

sort of money.'

'Thanks, Sally.'

'No offence intended, love,' was assured with a quick smile. 'Just saying he didn't need to offer it to you. So perhaps he was trying to be nice.'

Kate gave the other girl a look that asked whose side she was on before saying stubbornly, 'He probably knows I'm desperate.'

'Wouldn't that make it an even nicer gesture?' Sally argued but Kate was in no mood to appreciate logic.

'Not necessarily,' she replied. 'I bet he's interviewed a dozen girls already, only none of them were desperate enough to work for him.'

'Oh, I don't know. You mightn't like him, love, but he sounds an interesting character.'

'So was Ghenghis Khan,' Kate retorted drily, 'but I don't think he would have found many volunteers to type his memoirs either.'

Sally wasn't sure she was meant to laugh but she couldn't help herself. 'Oh, Kate, he can't be *that* bad.'

About to say he could, Kate restrained herself. She pulled a face, then smiled, showing her sense of humour hadn't entirely deserted her.

'Pity about the job though,' Sally resumed, slanting her a thoughtful look. 'That's a pretty good salary for a secretary, isn't it?'

'I'm afraid so,' Kate confirmed, well ahead of Sally.

'What does that mean?'

'Ever heard the expression—"an offer you can't refuse"?'

'Frequently,' Sally gave a short laugh. 'But at least this is an improvement on the ones I get down the club. You're going to take it?'

Kate grimaced. 'I suppose I am.'

'Cheer up, girl! For what it's worth,' Sally told her, 'I think you're being sensible.'

'Yes,' agreed Kate—only wishing she could afford not to be.

The following morning, her feelings hadn't changed. That same mixture of resignation and reluctance ensured she presented herself for work—but decidedly late.

She had no real excuse. Her alarm clock had gone off, the bus to Lancaster Gate had drawn up just as she'd arrived at the stop, and nothing had hindered her way through Kensington Gardens. Yet somehow she managed to lose half an hour during that walk in the park.

Even so, her mind was less occupied with inventing reasons for her lateness than visualising a scene in which Fitzgerald, infuriated by her obvious indifference to the fact, dismissed her on the spot. That way she'd not have to go through the however many days—hours—it took till they discovered working together was impossible.

She was still preoccupied with such thoughts when he answered the doorbell. He stared at her for a silent moment as he always did, then offered her his crooked smile.

'Good morning, Kate.'

She stared back at him, not saying anything, frowning as she waited for him to enact the correct scene of her imaginings.

And when he eventually asked, 'Something wrong?' she actually gave him a prompt.

'I'm late!' she announced boldly.

'Are you?' he murmured back with the complete indifference that should have been hers. Then with another smile, 'Well, I'll take your word for it. Mrs O'Reilly has just made some coffee. Come on through.'

Cheated was how Kate felt as she followed him to the kitchen. She thought of Howard scowling irritably if she was a minute late. Didn't Fitzgerald know how to treat his staff?

Apparently not. He waved her into the seat opposite his at the kitchen table, poured her coffee and asked, 'Want a bit of my newspaper?'

'I . . . er . . .' Kate said hesitantly.

'You're not going to bury your head in the paper, are you?' Mrs O'Reilly cut in briskly. 'Especially when you've got something better to look at this morning.'

'No, I guess not,' he conceded at this obvious reproof to his manners, and folding the offending paper, did exactly as ordered.

'No, really—I don't mind,' Kate stammered out after thirty seconds of his smiling scrutiny.

'Don't encourage him, dear.' The older woman eased her plump frame down on a chair and poured the coffee. 'Wastes half his life reading, he does. Not good for a body.'

'Ah, but what about the soul, Mrs O?' he quipped back.

'Not the sort of thing you read,' she dismissed with a sniff at the paper lying beside his plate.

Fitzgerald's lips twitched and Kate herself had to hide a smile behind her coffee cup. The paper was one of the most respectable nationals, making her wonder what sort of thing met with the other woman's approval. She was soon enlightened.

'Now the Bible. That's reading for the soul.'

'Amen,' Fitzgerald murmured under his breath and was awarded a stern look.

'He's lapsed, you know,' was confided to a puzzled Kate.

'Oh,' she replied, uncertain what else it might be appropriate to say.

'A lapsed Catholic,' Fitzgerald explained, then draining his cup, stood up. 'I think I'll take Kate away before you reveal all my worthless qualities.'

'Sure the day isn't long enough,' Mrs O'Reilly said, but with a decided twinkle in her eyes that made him chuckle.

'Does she always speak to you like that?' Kate asked when they were out in the hall corridor.

'Yeah, 'fraid so,' he laughed back. 'Mrs O sees it as part of her duties to care for my immortal soul as well as the housekeeping.'

'You don't mind?'

'Sure there's no harm in her,' he said, taking off the Southern Irish brogue to a tee and drawing Kate's first smile of the day.

It faded, however, as they entered the room next to the lounge. Obviously serving as a study, if the lounge had been untidy yesterday, at first glance this room was a disaster area.

'Mrs O doesn't come in here,' he said as she surveyed it.

'So I see,' Kate couldn't help muttering.

'She moves things,' was added by way of explanation.

Kate wondered if it was a subtle warning. No moving things! It shouldn't be too difficult to comply with. There didn't seem any vacant space left on either the desk or the crammed bookcases.

Then she noticed the smaller desk in the far corner by the window. In contrast to the rest of the room, it was neatly organised but her face fell when she realised what was sitting on it.

'Something wrong?' he asked for the second time that day.

Kate pointed at what looked like a small television with a keyboard attached. 'You expect me to use that?'

'It's a micro computer,' he said, guiding her over to the desk.

'I know *what* it is,' she bristled.

'Good.' He smiled and relayed with an air of satisfaction, 'The computer itself has a word processor facility, of course, and there's a printer you can use with it. The idea is you won't have to keep retyping my manuscript. You just run off a draft print, I mark it up and you simply insert the changes. That way you won't get bored with the book—well, not too bored anyway.'

He smiled again and waited for comment but Kate was still staring with horror at the array of equipment.

'I got it especially for you ... I thought you'd be pleased,' he went on at her silence.

He thought ... Kate was instantly sceptical. She slid him a sideways glance that caught the half-smile on his lips. In a flash of anger she imagined his *generosity* a planned exercise in her humiliation.

'I don't suppose it occurred to you that I might not know how to use it,' she retorted heavily.

'Oh, that's no problem,' he assured, apparently missing the accusation in her tone. 'The man in the store said it was child's play. You just type on the keyboard and the words come up on the screen.'

Kate knew *that* much already from listening to her

brother rambling on. And suddenly she had the distinct impression from Fitzgerald's vagueness, he knew little more himself. The equipment didn't even seem to be connected up, suggesting he hadn't tried to use it.

'Do I store what I've typed on that?' she asked, indicating a small black box beside the printer, and when he nodded, she picked up the cable attached to it. 'So where do I plug this in?'

'At the back somewhere I guess,' he said, peering behind the keyboard.

There was a line of sockets identified by initials. None were self-explanatory.

'Which one?' Kate pursued, beginning to enjoy herself as she watched him puzzling over it.

'It shouldn't be too difficult to figure out,' he replied with that irritating assurance of his.

'Good,' she echoed and quickly shielded the amusement in her eyes when he raised his head. Then while she waited with pleasurable anticipation for him to make a complete fool of himself, he lifted the instruction manual.

'Here you go.' He handed the book to her. 'Why don't I leave you to have a play on it?'

Why don't I ... Kate repeated to herself in the couple of seconds that it took to realise he intended to do just that.

'But——' she protested.

'Yes?' He turned at the door, and Kate would have had to be blind not to see the amusement in *his* eyes.

She gritted her teeth. 'Nothing!'

'See you later then,' he returned, his pleasantness mocking. 'Have fun!'

It required considerable restraint not to throw the manual after him. 'Swine!' she muttered under her breath, wondering if he always slid that easily out of awkward situations. Any other man would have at least tried to show her. Well, she would show him, Kate fumed, throwing herself down at the desk and flattening out the handbook.

In the beginning, its jargon seemed a foreign language to Kate who'd always shied away from anything technical. After a time, however, she discovered she'd absorbed a surprising amount of Johnny's lectures without being conscious of it. And adding that to what the book told her, she eventually worked out the basics.

Screen and typing keyboard connected, she copied the introductory paragraph from the manual and watched with delight as the text appeared on the screen.

Next she tackled storing the information on one of the small discs provided. That took longer because at first she inserted it into the slot in the box—'Sorry, disc drive,' she silently corrected—the wrong way round. But when she realised her mistake, it was a relatively simple operation.

And finally she concentrated on the printer, and found its instructions weren't that complicated either. It was more a matter of determination.

By the time he reappeared at noon, the printer was churning out the lines she'd typed.

'Congratulations,' he said with what she took to be sarcasm.

'As you said, it's not that difficult. In fact ...' she leaned over and read out the lines she'd printed, '... "Computers may seem intimidating to the inexperienced but they really are not so complicated. All that is required for a basic understanding of their usage is patience and a *modicum* of intelligence."'

The implication wasn't lost on him, of course, but she'd forgotten he was uninsultable.

Resting against the edge of the desk, a lazy grin on his face, he drawled, 'Do you think I stand a chance then?'

'I wouldn't know, Mr Fitzgerald.' She evaded the question by reverting to a chilly formality.

It had him switching to asking, 'How about calling me Van, huh?'

'I'd rather not,' she stated coolly.

'Why? You were on first name terms with Howard as I remember.'

'Yes, but I'd worked for him for a while,' she said, possibly a lame excuse.

'You'll be working for me a while too, I hope,' he argued back.

Did he really believe that? Kate wondered, glancing up at him with sceptical eyes. She still thought—as she had at the start of the day—working together was going to prove impossible. So far everything had reinforced the idea.

'I didn't hire you on a temporary basis, you know,' he continued, once more showing that uncomfortable ability to read her mind. 'Unlike Howard I have no plans to return to America in the future. So who can tell—if you play your cards right, you could still be with me in years to come.'

Thrilling prospect, Kate didn't think. He just had to be kidding. The smile pulling at the corners of his mouth suggested he was.

'In that case perhaps you could give me some work to get on with,' she replied, her own smile blatantly false, 'so I can impress you.'

'Oh, but you have already.' His look was slow and thorough and far too personal. 'Beautiful as well as smart. What more could a man ask for ... in a secretary?'

'Inexhaustible patience!' Kate snapped back as hers finally began to run out.

He chuckled. 'All right, sweet Kate. I'll get you my notes.'

He raked around on the cluttered desk until he found a folder. From its bulk it seemed the book was already half-written.

'You can start after lunch,' he said, placing it on her desk. 'I suppose you wouldn't consider sharing my meal with me.'

'You suppose correctly,' she echoed his dry tone. 'I've brought sandwiches.'

'Okay.' He shrugged and left her again.

Kate took twenty minutes over lunch and then turned her attention to his manuscript, with the same determination she'd applied to the computer. She might not wish him to think she was contemplating years of devoted service, but neither did she want to appear incompetent. It was a question of pride.

Her confidence, however, faltered as she flicked
through sheet after sheet of his draft. Every page was
covered with the same sprawling, untidy handwriting.
He didn't so much need a secretary, Kate thought in
despair, as an Egyptologist with a passion for
hieroglyphics. How could she possibly demonstrate her
efficiency when translating his appalling script alone
was going to take forever?

It took Kate the whole week to familiarise herself with
both the word processor and his handwriting, before
she could start typing at any speed. But if her painfully
slow progress bothered her, it didn't seem to worry
Fitzgerald. He simply shrugged and told her he was in
no hurry to finish the book.

In fact she barely saw him that first week. He did not
dictate his writing as Howard had, preferring to work
into the night, which according to Mrs O'Reilly,
accounted for his usual late hour of rising in the
morning. He also disappeared each afternoon for a
physiotherapy session at a London clinic, supporting
Kate's impression that his disability was recent. Again
according to Mrs O, the treatment was to strengthen the
muscles in his right leg although the limp would be
permanent. The Irish woman, however, said little about
his actual accident, referring to it in hushed tones as
'the tragedy'. She either assumed Kate knew all about it
or she found it a distressing subject.

At any rate, between his late risings and absences in
the afternoon, Kate had to suffer no more than the
occasional brief visit. But they were bad enough. He'd
come into the study, lean against her desk and make
increasingly provocative remarks until she could no
longer keep up a front of indifference. Then when he'd
got under her skin sufficiently for her cool reserve to
become a snapping exasperation, he would wander out
again, his irritating smile still in place. It was like a
game—a game she never quite mastered. Perhaps if
she'd understood its point, she might have. Or even
understood the man himself. But where she had found

Howard predictable and manageable most of the time, Van Fitzgerald defeated her completely.

He might appear one of the most easy-going employers, might smile a lot and show that irreverent sense of humour, might shrug when her own aloof response verged on rudeness, but she hadn't forgotten incidents that told of a different side to the man—a cruel harsh side that bore little resemblance to the 'lovely man' Mrs O'Reilly had claimed him to be. And which was truer to his nature became more and more difficult to judge, the further she got into his novel.

She wasn't sure what she'd expected—a blood and thunder thriller or a dry historical account of some war he'd reported as a correspondent. But it was neither.

At first it seemed very remote from a war story, the early chapters revolving around the childhoods of two American boys, one a farm boy from the Tennessee Backwoods, the other the son of a prominent banker. There was nothing romantic about the hand-to-mouth existence of Billy and his family, a hard lifestyle that had changed little in generations; and if Patrick was at the other extreme, growing up against a background of New England wealth, there was something unhealthy about the strict discipline exerted by an ambitious father. But Kate found her interest caught by the strong characterisation, so much so that she read on in her lunch hour.

And as the boys moved into late adolescence and events in their own very different worlds were dated by America's growing involvement in Vietnam, she realised any distancing was deliberate: such that when the two were finally called up for a war thousands of miles away in a country the farm boy had scarcely heard of, it was to appear an act of total insanity.

At least that was the way Kate interpreted the scene set by the time the two boys met up at the same army training camp. She didn't know whether she was reading it correctly for, unlike Howard, he did not expect any acknowledgement of his work, and if that suggested a total lack of interest in her opinion, she was, in the main, relieved. She wouldn't have lied yet she couldn't imagine herself offering an opinion in any objective way. Instead she suspected she would blurt out her incredulity—and ask him if he had really written the sensitive powerful prose disguised beneath the untidy, sprawling handwriting.

After a second week she managed to produce a respectable amount of proof for him to amend, and he asked her if she'd like to do some research. For once Kate's response was almost eager and he smiled at her enthusiasm. Then when she admitted to knowing very little about Vietnam, he armed her with a list of facts to check and patiently pointed her in the right direction.

She spent the next few days rushing round London from the American Embassy where officials seemed quite used to being asked odd questions, to the Foreign Office, where they were not; poring over history books in libraries; digging into newspaper archives and secretly loving every minute of it. When Van eventually asked her how she was getting on, she was able to present him with a neatly typed list of very comprehensive answers. And she couldn't help feeling a certain satisfaction at his comment of, 'You're a bright girl, Kate Gregory.'

She had a chance to impress him again when he started corresponding with a professor of history at the Sorbonne, an expert on the years of French rule in Vietnam. He'd already written to the professor but evidently the Frenchman did not have a great command of English and had replied in French. When Van asked her to find a translator, she volunteered her own services and removed the doubtful look from his face with a quick translation of the first page of the Professor's lengthy letter. Of course she cheated slightly, realising Van's French was almost non-existent, and later used a dictionary to ensure a totally accurate translation. But she enjoyed it too.

And gradually she discovered working for him was not impossible. Not even unpleasant. Exasperating sometimes, perhaps, when he was in one of his provocative moods, but he never behaved in the 'me boss, you slave' fashion Howard had.

Her wariness of him, however, remained even after a month had passed. The Van Fitzgerald she saw might kiss pretty girls for the hell of it, laugh his way out of tricky situations, charm his way into others, but it was certainly not the same Van Fitzgerald who wrote the poignant story of Patrick and Billy—and of all the American boys whose lives were changed, devastated, ended in a war that should never have been. And somehow Kate doubted he would want in his employ the daughter of a man who had made a fortune from dealing in arms, no matter if she had been ignorant of what had paid for her expensive schooling and pampered childhood, ignorant of how she had helped her father.

So if she grew to admire his work and to like the job, she still felt she had to maintain an aloof manner towards him. A manner that would discourage questions into her background, that would keep their relationship on a strictly impersonal basis.

Fortunately he didn't seem particularly anxious to put it on a different footing. Once he had asked her why she was being so 'hard-to-get-along-with', but it was a very casual remark, not demanding an answer. And the two times he'd enquired if she'd like to 'catch a bite to eat' with him, his approach had been equally casual, as was his acceptance of her quick excuses.

After that, she was unprepared for any serious invitations.

Certainly not one thrown at her in the middle of a letter he was dictating. In fact she'd actually written it down on her shorthand pad before she realised he couldn't possibly be asking the learned professor in Paris if he'd like to partner him at a dinner dance.

'Would I what?' she echoed, lifting her eyes to his.

'Accompany me to a dinner dance,' he repeated with a smile.

Surprised as she was, Kate's refusal was automatic. 'I'm sorry—I'm busy this weekend.'

Too automatic and probably expected, though he pursued, 'Otherwise you'd go?'

No, Kate thought, but she didn't consider it too diplomatic to say so outright.

'Perhaps,' she murmured.

'Then I'm in luck,' he drawled back, smile reappearing as he went on to explain, 'It's not at the weekend.'

Great, Kate thought, wondering how she was going to pick her diplomatic way out of that.

'What night is it?' She pretended to be genuinely interested.

He pretended to believe it. 'What nights are you free?'

She stopped pretending—she was damned if she was going to play guessing games and chance *her* luck.

'To be honest, I'd rather we kept our . . . association on its present basis.' Stiffly said but as a statement, it seemed self-explanatory. His silence, however, forced her to continue.

'And,' she stumbled on, 'I don't believe our socialising would be advisable. Not if we're to maintain a proper secretary-employer relationship.'

How Victorian it all sounded, Kate thought, cringing inwardly at her stilted words.

Apparently he thought so too.

'I say, Good Heavens, Miss Gregory,' he returned with a very fair imitation of a very stuffy English accent, 'what can you think I'm asking of you? It was as my secretary I was inviting you to go.'

'It was?'

'Yeah,' he said in his own voice, straight-faced, if lying through his teeth. 'And *naturally* I intend to pay you overtime for the duty.'

Was that meant to be tempting? Kate wondered, feeling rather insulted instead. It reminded her too much of the wrong impression he'd once had of the *social* duties she'd performed for his friend Howard.

'Wouldn't it be cheaper to ask one of your girlfriends?' she muttered back.

'Girlfriends?' He gave her a quizzical look.

Who it was intended to fool, Kate didn't know, as she pointed out, 'I take some of your calls, remember?'

As well as a Barbara, he appeared to know an Aimi, a Jill and an Ellen—at the last count. Admittedly the

Ellen had turned out to be his sister who also lived on this side of the Atlantic with her English husband.

'Mere friends,' he corrected with a wry smile. 'And even if I wanted to ask one of them, I doubt they would enjoy the affair. It's an awards dinner for the Society of Political and Economic Journalists—a serious-minded lot on the whole. Most of the women I used to date before this would be bored stupid just sitting and talking all evening.'

'Surely it won't be that dull if it's a dinner dance,' she argued back.

'Perhaps not for some,' he conceded, 'but you're forgetting that my dancing days are over.'

Kate had—completely. It was days—weeks—since she'd even noticed his limp. It was just part of him, a totally insignificant part, overshadowed by other characteristics like his maddening humour. And she doubted his lady friends would consider it important either.

But when she looked at him now, she suddenly wondered if he ever forgot. Something in his eyes suggested he didn't. Although he had never mentioned it before, she had the oddest feeling he was testing her, waiting for some reaction.

'I had forgotten actually,' she admitted on a deliberately offhand note, 'and I wouldn't have thought it mattered that much.'

'Exactly—*you* wouldn't,' he echoed, changing the stress of her words. 'In fact I'm sure you would find dancing with me a positive deterrent. Which is why I'm inviting you, my *social* secretary, instead of someone who might anticipate enjoying the evening.'

'I see,' Kate muttered coldly—no more pleased now she realised the invitation had been on a strictly impersonal basis. 'You're paying me to be bored.'

'If you must put it like that,' he replied, his eyes narrowing. 'Listen, all I'm asking is your company for an evening at an extremely formal occasion. But if that's too much, then I'm sure I can stand a few odd looks and go on my own.'

Did *he* have to put it like that? Kate thought in turn,

picking up the sulky note in his voice. She'd never heard it before and she wasn't altogether sure she wasn't being manipulated by Mr Van Fitzgerald into feeling sorry for him.

Successfully manipulated. 'Is it evening dress?'

'Yes,' he confirmed.

'When?'

'Tomorrow night,' he went on, his lazy smile quickly—far too quickly—back in place. 'Short notice, I know, but I was reluctant to go myself.'

That made two of them, Kate thought, but she found herself nodding when he asked if she were free.

CHAPTER SEVEN

'You look fabulous!' Sally declared as Kate circled for her. 'That has got to be *the* most gorgeous dress I have ever seen.'

'You don't think it looks dated?' Kate frowned.

The dress was certainly special—a sumptuous designer gown with a dark blue velvet bodice and long, flowing, taffeta skirt in a lighter blue threaded with gold—but it was also more than two years old.

'Don't be daft!' Sally laughed at her anxiety. 'It has what we in the trade call timeless elegance. And the velvet choker looks just right ... better than heavy jewellery in my opinion.'

'Yes, it is nice,' Kate agreed, fingering the dark blue band that matched her dress. 'But I still feel rather bare. Perhaps I should put my hair down.'

'Not on your life!' Sally exclaimed, defending the way she herself had coiled Kate's lustrous black hair in a style that matched the dress's sophistication. 'The whole point of a strapless gown like this *is* to show off those beautiful bones of yours.'

'Yes, but——' Kate took another glance in the mirror at her slender shoulders and the slight swell of her breasts visible, wondering if she was exposing too much.

'Honestly, Kate,' her friend read the doubts flitting across her face, 'any man in his right mind would be proud to be seen with you. And crazy though your boss is, I bet he won't be an exception.'

Kate wasn't so confident about predicting his reaction but she smiled. 'Thanks, Sally. For the moral support—and the loan of the shawl, of course. It's lovely.'

'My pleasure, only don't hide under it all evening will you?' Sally teased as she watched Kate carefully draping the gold-coloured silk to cover as much as possible.

'It might be cold,' Kate suggested almost hopefully.

'At the Royal Maitland?' Sally raised her eyes heavenwards. '*Kate*, it's got to be one of the plushest joints in town—as well as being too respectable for even your American to make a lunge.'

'A lunge?' Kate echoed the Northern girl's slang and then working out its meaning, protested, 'Really, Sally, how many times have I told you he's only invited me because he doesn't want to inflict a very boring evening on any of his girlfriends?'

'Oh, about ten,' Sally replied, lips quirking in amusement. 'So when's he picking you up?'

'He's not. The hotel isn't that far from his flat so it seemed pointless him travelling all the way over here,' Kate justified her own refusal to let him. 'It's quicker to get a taxi and meet him there.'

In the end, however, Kate found she'd cut things too fine. Fate and every traffic light between Notting Hill and the Royal Maitland conspired to make her over twenty minutes late.

Luckily when a young porter showed her to the private bar off the ballroom, the pre-dinner drinking was still in full swing. Craning her neck, she searched for a glimpse of his familiar blond head and was relieved when she saw him threading his way through the crowd.

'Kate, I thought you weren't——'

'I know I'm late but——'

They'd started speaking together and they both broke off with a short laugh.

'You first,' Kate offered but whatever Fitzgerald had been about to say was forgotten as the borrowed shawl slipped from her shoulders. And he was silent so long, she began to think the peculiar expression in his eyes must be horror.

'You did say an evening gown,' she reminded defensively, 'and this is the only one I've got. I'm sorry if you don't consider it suitable.'

'Suitable?' he echoed, tone dazed. 'Hell it's . . . you're . . .'

He seemed to get lost in staring again, only this time Kate felt an unexpected pleasure at having achieved the impossible—rendered Fitzgerald speechless!

He himself was wearing a dinner suit, a radical change from his usual jeans and casual shirts, but he carried it off so well with his tall, muscular frame, she found herself having to make a conscious effort *not* to stare at him.

'Goddamn devastating!' he eventually managed with a laugh that mocked his unusual loss for words.

'Thank you.' She inclined her head in acknowledgement, returning politely, 'Actually you look rather . . . distinguished yourself, Mr Fitzgerald.'

'Distinguished, mm? Why I do believe that's the nicest thing you've ever said to me, sweet Kate,' he teased before guiding her through the crowd. He received several greetings on the way, evidently well-known among this circle of journalists. Kate began to feel nervous, very much an outsider. Finally they reached the far side of the bar to join a middle-aged couple, standing in one corner.

'This is Kate,' he announced, as though he'd already mentioned her to his friends.

'Pleased to meet you,' she murmured shyly, conscious of their interested stares.

'Barbara Davies.' The woman took over the introduction with a smile, then a wry glance at the man beside her, 'And this bug-eyed monster is for better and sometimes worse, my husband Owen . . . Stop staring at the poor girl, Owen, and say hello.'

'Sorry, was I? Yes, I suppose I was,' the man admitted with an abashed grin.

'Like a hawk,' his wife added but her expression suggested she was amused rather than annoyed by the fact. 'Don't let it embarrass you, Kate. You know what these middle-aged men are like.'

'*Middle-aged!*—I resent that,' Owen protested with mock indignation and the others laughed.

'Owen used to be an editor of mine,' Van relayed to Kate.

'Sub-editor, and one of many,' Owen corrected modestly, and at her obvious puzzlement, explained, 'Our man here is strictly freelance. Which is just as well because to my knowledge he's fallen out with every editor in the business at some time or other.'

Kate could believe *that* but the other woman rushed to his defence. 'Only because they're such egotists, eh, Van?'

'Megalomaniacs,' he confirmed gravely.

'The very word.' Barbara looked askance at her husband who appeared to be taking the ribbing with good humour.

'Don't listen to them, Kate. I'm really the mildest of men,' he said, eyes twinkling behind heavy-framed spectacles. 'Now tell me, how long have you known our Yankee friend?'

'I've worked for Mr Fitzgerald about a month,' Kate replied quietly, still feeling some shyness.

'*Mr* Fitzgerald?' Owen's eyebrows rose humorously.

And gently mocking, Van inserted, 'Kate believes in preserving the formalities.'

'Oh, but I thought——' Owen looked at Kate in surprise. 'Then you're just . . .'

'My secretary, I'm afraid so,' Van supplied with an air of feigned regret.

'Lord, I thought——'

'Yes, Owen,' his wife cut in, observing Kate's deepening frown, 'we've all guessed what you thought.'

Her tone was very dry but Van's was more an amused drawl as he went on, 'After you insisted I came to this shindig, I had problems finding a partner at short notice and Kate here took pity on me. Didn't you, Kate?'

'Yes,' she confirmed almost curtly—somehow he'd managed to make the truth sound ridiculous!

Apparently Owen found it so, laughing back, 'I can scarcely believe that, Van. I seem to remember a time when you——'

'Owen *darling*,' Barbara interrupted again, the endearment covering a sharp dig in his ribs, 'people seem to be going in. Why don't you lead the way to our table?'

Owen looked perplexed, knowing he must have said something wrong, but Barbara took his arm before he could add to his indiscretion.

The younger couple followed a pace behind and Van used the opportunity to murmur, 'Now you've established the basis of our relationship, do you think you could relax a little?'

'What do you mean?' said Kate, immediately defensive. 'I merely told Owen how long I'd worked for you.'

'Yes, well . . . if you could manage to dispense with the *respectful* Mr Fitzgeralds, it would be greatly appreciated,' he drawled back.

Despite the sarcasm, Kate saw his point. But because of it, she wasn't about to tell him her stiffness was due to nerves. Instead she lapsed into a sullen silence as he led her into the ballroom where the dinner was to be held.

As Sally had said, it had an extremely luxurious atmosphere, the long tables laid with glittering silverware and glass and arranged on three sides of a highly polished floor, lit by hanging chandeliers. Their table was set for six couples and they were the last to be seated; Kate found herself next to Owen and a younger man called Tom. The lively level of chatter suggested most people at the table already knew each other and from the warm way Van was greeted, he too was a familiar figure.

Perhaps she should have realised he had been pulling her leg about his friends. After all, he himself was hardly the dullest of individuals. She watched him now—talking to Barbara and another journalist, grinning at something said, making them laugh with his wry reply. He was so obviously well-liked that after a while Kate could see why. He never dominated a conversation but his easy-going charm and humour were infectious, his refusal to take himself seriously an attractive quality.

When her neighbour, Tom, asked, 'So how's that book going?' he might have looked very grave for a moment, as though considering a weighty reply.

But he confined himself to a dry, 'Slowly,' which elicited general laughter as intended.

To his credit, he was also an attentive partner, possibly recognising her reserve for shyness and including her in conversation until she became relaxed with his friends. Even when they were both talking to other people, from time to time he would glance across the table and smile. And gradually she didn't find it that much of a strain to answer those fleeting smiles.

The awards ceremony took place directly after the dinner. Discovering she'd actually enjoyed the meal, Kate wondered if this might be the tedious part Van had threatened. The presentations, however, turned out to be less staged than most and the acceptance speeches, by and large, more interesting. At least she managed to listen with polite attention up until the second last award and a speech by a rather pompous economics journalist which was as boring as it was long.

Stifling a yawn, Kate caught Fitzgerald's grin and, almost together, they both raised their eyes to the ceiling and then smiling, back to one another.

And Kate decided she must have had too much wine over dinner because suddenly she felt that strong pull of attraction she'd first experienced at Howard's party. A dangerous feeling she'd ignored since and tried to ignore now.

Nevertheless, her eyes returned to him when the speech was finally over and the polite clapping tailed off. He was still looking at her—no longer smiling but with an oddly intent expression which had nothing to do with the ceremony.

That was evident for there was no flicker of response in his steady gaze as the announcer continued, '. . . perhaps the most prestigious in British journalism although this year it goes to a foreigner. However, I use that term very much tongue in cheek because the man in question has been around so long most of us have tended to overlook that transatlantic drawl of his. At any rate, I take great pleasure in presenting this award for his account of the civil war in Bowchasa—indeed for a decade of the most outstanding journalism— to . . .'

And there was no pretence in Van Fitzgerald's look of blank astonishment when his name being announced finally penetrated that distraction. In fact, for a couple of seconds while an immediate clamour of applause broke out round the room, it seemed he couldn't quite take in what was happening, his thoughts had been so far away.

It was Owen who helped him out by leaning across the table to take and pump his hand in congratulations. 'The Messenger, man,' he beamed, naming the particular award. 'Quite a surprise, eh?'

There was a decided twinkle in Owen's eyes that suggested it was no such thing to him at least.

And undeceived, Van murmured under cover of the applause, 'When I get back, I'm going to murder you, Owen boy,' before leaving his chair to collect the award.

'I think he means it,' Owen laughed to Kate who was also rather bewildered by events.

'You knew, didn't you?' she said, and a broad grin confirmed it.

'I was deputised to make sure he attended this year,' he admitted. 'If he'd been told about the award beforehand, wild horses wouldn't have dragged him here.'

Kate wondered why as she watched him shake the hand of the newspaper baron presenting the awards, and without any sign of nerves, step up to the microphone for his acceptance speech.

'Ladies and gentlemen,' he began when the clapping

eventually died down, 'I am truly honoured to receive this award—especially at this time. As some of you may know, I have recently retired from your ranks. The Messenger,' he raised the silver statue in his hand, 'will serve as a reminder of all the fine people I have met over the years.

'Once—a lifetime ago it seems—I was destined to be a slick Washington lawyer. I shall be eternally grateful that the course of my life was altered. For if sometimes I have felt my words inadequate, I have always believed in what we try to do—shall always be proud to have been one of you. For this award and that privilege, I thank you.'

The briefest speech of the evening, but its sincerity was unquestionable and the applause was deafening.

Kate found herself clapping as loudly as anyone, and watching men rise from their tables to take his hand, she was reminded of the way Howard had once described him—as 'a man worth knowing'. And suddenly she felt the strangest sense of loss, realising *she* did not really know him at all.

He was detained at a table by one man and Owen muttered with mild contempt, 'Trust Cutler. I bet he's offering him a job.'

'Cutler?' Kate echoed.

'Editor of one of the Sundays. He's probably fool enough to offer Van a sub-editorship.'

'That's bad?' She seemed to remember it was Owen's own position.

'Not for someone who likes the quiet life, perhaps,' he conceded with a wry smile, 'but Van was first, last and always a field correspondent. He may have accepted his disability rules that out now, but I very much doubt he would see a desk job as compensation.'

'How long has it been since his accident?' Kate asked.

A natural enough question she would have thought, but it drew a puzzled look from Owen and then an oddly flat reply of, 'Van wasn't in any accident.'

'But I was told——' she paused and changed to saying, '—least I assumed he was injured in a car crash or something.'

'No, nothing like that.' Owen was clearly reluctant to say more but Kate stared at him until he sighed. 'All right, maybe you ought to be aware of how it happened. You see about six months ago, while the rest of the world was concentrating on the Lebanon, Van was in Bowchasa, a small republic in West Africa, reporting an equally bloody civil war. Unfortunately, when his stories began to attract attention, the official regime decided they didn't like it. So some government troops took him into the bush, supposedly on a reconnaissance, and shot him. He was left for dead but a guerilla force picked him up and managed to patch his stomach wound. They made rather a mess of setting his leg, however, and by the time he was well enough to be smuggled out of the country, the damage was permanent . . .' Owen finally trailed off, voice roughened by emotion.

Kate remained silent, shocked by the violence of the story and shaken by how painful she found the image of Van close to death.

'I shouldn't have talked so much.' Owen sighed heavily, noticing her paleness. 'Van will definitely murder me if he hears I've been telling you gory tales.'

'He never mentioned it,' she replied faintly.

'Yes, well, you know Van,' Owen said as though it explained everything.

But Kate again thought, 'I don't—not at all.'

'There's no chance of him going back to that kind of work, is there?' she asked, conscious of willing the answer to be 'no'.

'If he wanted to, he could. Being freelance, it's his choice,' Owen replied frankly. 'And though he says he's retired now, I only hope he *can* settle for something else.'

'He has his writing,' Kate pointed out.

'Maybe,' Owen said on a doubtful note, 'but Van's too powerful a writer to waste his time turning out pulp fiction. And always supposing he is successful, I can't imagine what sort of satisfaction he'd gain from it. After all, with his background he hardly needs to make the bestseller list,' Owen finished with a wry chuckle.

That chuckle, however, was the last straw for Kate, struggling to keep her temper at such a dismissive attitude. 'Well, *I'm* positive he will be successful,' she stated emphatically. 'And you mightn't consider fiction as important, but I think you're wrong. A novel like Van's will reach more people than any dry, factual newspaper account ever could. I mean really reach them—change hearts as well as minds, and that's what counts!'

Owen was plainly taken aback by her outburst and when she finally ran out of steam, so was Kate. What was she doing? Van Fitzgerald didn't need her championing his work.

She realised that even before she looked away from Owen's now curious expression to discover, with a sickening jolt, they had at some stage gained an audience.

For a moment Kate simply stared at Van in horror, every impulsive word she'd uttered echoing through her head. Then she dropped her eyes to the tablecloth, blushing furiously and desperately wishing herself somewhere else—anywhere but under his speechless gaze.

Owen was the only one equal to the situation, as he greeted, 'Van—we were just discussing your book. You appear to have an ardent admirer in Kate here.'

'So I heard,' was murmured back in a distracted voice.

'Not in any detail, of course,' Owen rambled on after a stricken look from Kate. 'I'm afraid I was showing a certain lack of faith in you and she was putting me right. Very eloquently, too. You should consider yourself lucky to have a—secretary like her.'

'Oh, I do,' Van said in a tone of such indulgence Kate couldn't help staring at him again. Only this time, he was actually smiling—no, grinning. Not annoyed at all. Pleasantly amused if anything, as, holding her eyes, he murmured to the older man, 'And I wouldn't part with her so don't get any ideas, Owen.'

'Ah, if only I could,' the Welshman's sigh was wistful, 'but with the late hours I sometimes do, it's more politic to have a battleaxe of about fifty. You know how suspicious wives can be.' The last was obviously intended for Barbara as she turned from conversation with another couple.

'I hope you don't believe this husband of mine.' She fixed a baleful eye on Owen, 'I think for that remark, my love, you can do your penance on the dance floor.'

From his groan, dancing was plainly not Owen's favourite pastime but he took the hint and stood up for the next waltz.

'They're nice,' Kate said shyly when the older couple had excused themselves.

'Yes,' Van agreed. 'And you've obviously made quite an impression on Owen.'

Good or bad? Kate wondered but decided not to ask, all too aware that a general shifting to the bar and the dance floor had left them alone at the table.

Instead she murmured, 'Congratulations, by the way,' indicating his award, a small statue in silver representing Mercury, the messenger of the gods.

'Thanks,' he smiled back, a certain wryness recognising the deliberate change of subject.

'You were obviously not expecting it,' she pursued.

He shook his head. 'No, though I should have guessed Owen was up to something. It's not the first time that Welshman's landed me in an awkward situation.'

'He probably knew you'd be able to talk your way out of it,' Kate replied on a slightly dry note.

Picked up by Van as he drawled back, 'I can't decide if that's an insult or a compliment.'

'I just meant you made a good speech,' she claimed more innocently.

'Mm.' He seemed less than convinced. 'Well, I'll take your word for it. To be honest, I don't quite recall what I said.'

'You weren't nervous?' she asked incredulously.

'Don't you believe it,' he chuckled back. 'I've hated making speeches ever since I was a kid and I stammered all the way through my first. As I recall, I only had a few lines to say but I fouled up so badly, I was almost crying by the end.'

Kate was unable to suppress a smile at this unlikely image. 'A school speech, you mean.'

'No, it was at one of my father's rallies,' he replied with a dry laugh and seeing she was puzzled, explained, 'He was running for election to the Senate—for the first time if I remember correctly. Anyway, I was supposed to do my little Lord Fauntleroy act and promote his family image.'

Kate frowned as he broke off to light a cigarette. Though his words were humorous enough, there had been a slightly bitter note in his voice.

'Did he win?' she allowed herself a little curiosity.

'Despite my efforts, yes. Or maybe I got him the sympathy vote for having an idiot son.' He laughed—a definitely bitter sound this time.

'Was he very angry about it?'

He shrugged before continuing wryly, 'Well, he didn't yell at me or anything. That's not my father's style. But after he'd ignored me at the dinner table for a week, I got the hint he wasn't overpleased with my performance.'

Kate was reminded of her own father, the coldness of his anger, and she murmured, 'You don't like him very much, do you?'

He smiled at the very English understatement as he admitted, 'Not very much, no. To be honest, I haven't seen him in about thirteen years. He wrote me off when I became a correspondent after I'd finished my tour of duty in Vietnam.'

Thinking of his speech, Kate concluded, 'He wanted you to be a lawyer.'

'Not as such. That was more a starting point from which to enter politics. But yes, he had very different plans for me.'

'You didn't share them?'

'Oh, I went along.' His mouth twisted with a touch of self-mockery. 'In fact, I spent the first twenty-three years of my life going along with them. But after law school I was drafted for Vietnam and then, I guess I would say, I discovered there were worse things in the world than my father's displeasure . . .' He shook his head as he trailed off and gave a dismissive laugh. 'Hell, I don't know why I'm boring you with all this stuff—even if I am paying you for the privilege.'

'Do you have to put it like that?' she almost snapped, a reversal of the day before's conversation.

'Sorry, just kidding.' He grinned. 'I would sooner talk about more interesting matters though.'

'Like what?' she queried suspiciously.

'Oh, like you, maybe,' he returned to Kate's dismay. 'Do you realise I don't know much more about you than your name?'

Kate realised it and intended to keep things that way. 'I'm afraid I've led a very dull life compared with you, Mr Fitzgerald.'

Her sudden reversion to his surname was noted with a wry, 'I get the feeling I'm being told to mind my own business again.'

Unsure how to answer, Kate was relieved to see some of the others returning. Van, however, didn't seem to welcome the interruption. He stood up and walking round to her side of the table, murmured, 'Come on.'

With little choice but to take his hand, Kate initially assumed they were heading towards the bar. Even when he finally halted at the edge of the dance floor in the far corner from their table, his intention still hadn't got through to her. It wasn't until he turned and put an arm at her waist, she caught on and actually recoiled in her surprise.

An unsubtle reaction she compounded with an incredulous, 'You want to dance?'

'That was the general idea,' he drawled back. 'I would have asked you at the table only I had the feeling you might just stand there, staring up at me with those big brown eyes of yours.'

Which was exactly what she was doing now, his mocking words made Kate realise. She stopped gaping at him but muttered, 'I thought you said your dancing days were over.'

'I've changed my mind.' He placed a hand at her waist

again and smiled. 'Don't worry, I won't stand on your feet.'

'I wasn't worried about that.' She frowned as he began to guide her in a slow circle round the floor.

'Yes, I know,' he replied quietly. 'However, I'm sure I can manage to shuffle to this.'

Nervously Kate waited for him to continue their earlier conversation but, pulling her closer, he lapsed into silence.

One dance merged into another as they circled to the soft romantic music played when the hour is late. He drew her even closer, resting his cheek against her hair. And if Kate thought she should break away, she felt no resentment at the way he held her, a hand lightly caressing her back, the other clasping hers. Round and round they danced until they were simply swaying to the music under the dimmed lights.

'You're not falling asleep on me, are you?' Van eventually whispered, his lips touching her brow as she moved her head. 'Tired?'

'A little.'

'Then I'd better get you home. We wouldn't want you to be late for work, would we?' he said with feigned sternness.

'No, sir,' she answered pertly, suddenly no longer guarding every reply.

They made their farewells to the rest and when they emerged from the hotel, a doorman offered to call them a taxi. Unexpectedly Van shook his head and taking her arm, started to walk along the pavement.

Kate smiled quizzically. 'If you're thinking of walking me home, Mr Fitzgerald, I live thataway.'

'You know I haven't walked a girl home in years,' he said reminiscently, without taking any notice of her direction.

'It's also beginning to rain,' she pointed out.

He held a hand palm upward. 'So it is. In that case, we'd better make a run for it.'

'It' turned out to be a brand new saloon car parked round the corner from the hotel. Kate recognised it as a Mercedes Benz—a top of the range model.

'That's yours?' she asked—rather stupidly because he was already opening a door for her.

'Nice, isn't it?' he said, patting the beautiful coachwork with pride of ownership. 'I was declared fit and able to drive last week so I bought it to celebrate. In you get.'

Kate sank into the upholstery, a plush tan suede. 'Very nice,' she said when he was behind the wheel, 'but it must have cost a fortune.'

He glanced at her in surprise and it struck Kate what her comment implied. She might as well have come right out and asked if he could afford a car like this.

It appeared to amuse him though as he teased, 'Don't worry. I have it on good authority that my book's going to be an enormous success.'

She gave him a stony look. 'I didn't say enormous and I don't think it's very gentlemanly to cast up a person's *weak* moments to them.'

'Ah, that was what it was—a weak moment,' he repeated with a grin but at her even stonier glance, decided against following it up and instead turned to start the car.

On the journey home, however, Kate found herself murmuring, 'Owen seemed to think you might go back to your correspondence work.'

'I'm not planning on it,' he shrugged in reply.

It didn't sound a very definite answer and she added, 'Do you miss it?'

'At times,' he admitted after a moment's thought. 'But over the years I'd lost much of my first conviction that you could change opinion by simply reporting the horrors of war. Too much horror and people switch off.'

'Yes,' she agreed quietly, then pursued, 'So you won't be going back?'

They'd reached a set of traffic lights and Van glanced sideways to catch her worried expression. 'Would it bother you if I did, sweet Kate?'

Feeling he was mocking her concern, Kate answered flippantly, 'Yes, of course. I would be out of a job, wouldn't I?'

He winced slightly before laughing under his breath, 'I guess I asked for that.'

Then they moved away from the lights and Kate spent the rest of the journey determinedly ignoring him. He found her street without direction and, parking in the first car space near her flat, walked her the few yards to the door.

'I suppose you wouldn't consider offering me a cup of coffee,' he said after she'd retrieved her keys from the bottom of her handbag.

Kate didn't find the question that unexpected but she hesitated too long, searching for a tactful refusal.

'Great.' He accepted her silence as an invitation and taking the key from her hand, added like a perfect gentleman, 'Here. Let me do that for you.'

They were in the hallway before Kate had recovered enough of her wits to stammer an excuse, 'Look, my place is in an awful mess and——'

'I don't mind.' He shrugged and used the second key on the ring.

Considering his own untidiness, he probably didn't, but when Kate went in first to switch on the light, she was appalled to find the flat in an even worse state than she'd remembered. She'd been given the day off to prepare for the dinner party and had used some of it to sort through clothes that needed mending as well as various forgotten items she'd promised to send on to Johnny. Only she hadn't got round to tidying them away in her last-minute rush.

She shut her eyes in the hope that when she opened them, the mess would have disappeared.

Instead she heard Van's voice drawling, 'My God, I think I've found a soulmate,' as he took in the chaos of her flat.

'It's not usually this bad—*really*,' she stated defensively, not sharing his amusement at all as she began to hastily clear up some of the junk.

'It's okay, leave it,' he said, still on a note of laughter, but it served to make an embarrassed Kate more frantic in her efforts to bring order. And with a heap of clothes scooped in her arms, she cannoned right into him as he left the door. He steadied her and repeated firmly, 'I said leave it.'

'It won't take me——' she started and gasped as she found her bundle being tossed unceremoniously on the sofa.

'Dammit, Kate, must you always argue,' he said on a growl of exasperation. 'There's a time for fighting and a time for . . . well, for other things.'

Other things? Kate repeated to herself and was almost stupid enough to repeat it aloud. But she caught the way he was looking at her and then didn't have to ask. It was in his eyes suddenly without laughter, the hands reaching out for her, fingers closing gently on her bare arms. Drawing her nearer yet giving her all the time in the world to back away, to shake her head, to say one word in protest.

But if she did eventually it wasn't altogether surprising it had little effect—her 'no' sounding disturbingly like the opposite as his lips brushed lightly on her forehead and he murmured, 'Just a kiss, Kate,' before his mouth claimed hers, soft and persuasive until her lips began to part for him and he raised a hand to hold her head still.

Then she couldn't protest any more for the kiss suddenly changed, became hard and demanding, robbing her of words and breath and finally any reason at all. Instinctively her arms slid round his neck, her fingers tangling in his hair, and he gave a deep groan of satisfaction because he knew he no longer had to hold her captive for his kiss.

The shawl had long since slipped to the floor, leaving much of her back bare to hands rough against her softer skin yet gentle in their movement. His mouth left hers and trailed down her throat till it kissed the erratic pulse at its base, beating with a mixture of pleasure and desire and fear.

Barely conscious of her dress zip sliding down her back, it was pleasure that made her gasp when she first felt his hand on the swell of her breast. Desire that made her moan, soft and sweet, as sensitive fingers sought and found its peak, teased gently and excited unbearably. But fear that made her at last resist.

A fear that shivered through her as his other hand shaped her hips to a hard muscular frame that unashamedly revealed his own arousal, and he groaned against her hair, 'I want you so much, Kate. So very much . . .'

'No, Van!' She tried to twist free, and her sudden cry sounded what it was—pure panic.

Panic that grew as he set her back from him, with eyes first incredulous, then angry. Eyes in which desire did not die as they shifted to the flesh his fingers had already exposed, but hardened into a crueler kind of passion that had her stammering almost incoherently, 'I-I haven't ever . . . I m-mean I don't . . .'

Not thinking he would understand, Kate's gaze widened in appeal as she watched the changing expressions on his face, a confusion of emotions she couldn't read. And she trembled when he drew her to him again, although his hands were gentle.

'Don't be scared, Kate, please,' he murmured softly as he stroked her bare back once before sliding her dress zip in place. 'I was just angry for a second because I didn't realise why you got so frightened. I wouldn't hurt you. I just wanted to . . . well, I guess that was obvious. But I'd never force you, Kate, believe me.'

Kate did believe him, so much so that his quiet apology made her ashamed of her own behaviour, and cheeks warm with embarrassment, she mumbled, 'I'm sorry. I shouldn't have let you . . .'

'It wasn't your fault, Kate,' he insisted, his voice grave and wholly unfamiliar in its seriousness. 'I was going too fast again but now I know . . . know how absurdly wrong I was in ever believing Howard, things will be different. I can wait until . . . well, until maybe you feel the same.' He chose his words carefully but Kate already felt she was being rushed into something.

She stared back at him, uncertain how to reply, wishing they could simply pretend the last few minutes had never happened.

Van sensed her withdrawing from him. 'Look, why

don't you make us that coffee and we can talk about it?'
he suggested quickly.

Kate nodded, grateful for an excuse to retreat to the
small curtained-off kitchen. She heard him settling down
on the creaking springs of the ancient armchair and
desperately tried to think of a way to retreat from the
whole situation. Not finding one, she continued to stand
in the kitchen till steam from the kettle filled the air.

Then suddenly Fitzgerald appeared in the doorway to
ask with biting sarcasm, 'Do you wear this?'

He was holding out a striped tie, Johnny's spare
school one. 'No, it's my——'

'Then how about the man's shirts in the wardrobe?'
he pursued, cutting across her reply.

'You've been looking inside my wardrobe?' Kate
demanded indignantly.

'It was open.' There was no suggestion of excuse in
his tone. 'I wanted to see if the tie I found lying on the
sofa was a one-off. But it's not, is it?'

Kate saw the conclusions he'd already drawn in the
look of contempt he threw her and was momentarily
speechless.

'I shouldn't bother stretching your imagination for a
perfectly innocent explanation,' he continued, mistaking
the cause of her silence, 'I can use my own.'

'Yes, and we all know how reliable that is!' Kate
snapped back, but its implication was lost on him.

'However, I think I deserve a reason why you didn't
tell me you were heavily involved elsewhere—instead of
putting on that cute little virgin act,' he ground out,
throwing the tie so it landed on the work surface beside
her.

'And when was I supposed to tell you—before or
after you made that *clumsy* pass at me?' Kate enquired
just as furious and hitting out at his male vanity.

'*Before* you started driving me crazy with those sweet
little moans of yours,' he bit back, reminding her of
how intitially responsive she had been to his far from
clumsy advances. 'Or is that how you get your kicks—
turning a man on till he's ready to make a fool of
himself for you?'

'Oh, you don't need my help for that, Mr Fitzgerald,' returned Kate with sneering derision.

'*Mr* Fitzgerald,' he echoed on an explosive note. 'So we're back to playing the proper little secretary, are we? Well, in that case, *Miss* Gregory, I suggest you remember who *is* boss round here the next time you open your goddamn, prissy, English mouth!'

It took Kate a moment to grasp the nature of the threat and for another she simply stared at him in total astonishment. But when she did eventually reply, it was to retort scathingly, 'Mr Fitzgerald, for all I care, you can take yourself and your job and your bloody stupid book, and go straight back to Bow—Bow—whatever its name was!'

'It's called the Central Republic of Bowchasa, Miss Gregory—and since that sounds more like your honest opinion of my book, perhaps it might be better if I do just that!' The fury in his final words left Kate stunned. Too late did she realise how deeply she had—must have—hurt him with her thoughtless barb. For he had turned away as he spoke and, without even a backward glance, slammed the door behind him.

And too late, did Kate choke out the words, 'I didn't mean it.'

CHAPTER EIGHT

KATE was still in her nightgown when she opened her door to Sally some two days later. They hadn't seen each other since the night of the dinner dance because Sally had been away on a modelling assignment.

'I thought I heard the radio. Day off?' the other girl asked but didn't pause for an answer before running on with breathless excitement, 'Have you seen it?'

'Seen what?'

'Your photograph—in one of the dailies no less. Here, top right of the gossip page.' Sally handed the newspaper she was waving to a bemused Kate and quoted the caption beneath the grimy photograph, '"Michael Fitzgerald the Third and companion". It is you, isn't it?'

'Yes, I suppose so,' Kate murmured although she didn't remember the picture being taken and if it was a good likeness of Fitzgerald, her face was a shadowy profile.

'Is all that stuff true then?' Sally pursued.

Kate read the opening sentences. 'Yes, he won an award at the dinner.'

'Not that bit.' Sally dismissed the ostensible reason for the picture. 'The other part, further down—about his family.'

Puzzled, Kate's eyes returned to the article, scanned it once and with a growing sense of disbelief, read more slowly the significant paragraph.

'As well as being a celebrated journalist, Michael Sullivan Fitzgerald is from one of the first families in Boston. Educated at the famous Leyton Military Academy and later Harvard, he is the son of the influential senator of the same name and is rumoured to have inherited a considerable personal fortune from his maternal grandfather, Samuel Joyce, a former president of Rymer's, one of the most powerful merchant banks in America. Despite this background Van, as he is more commonly known, seems to favour our shores along with his sister, Lady Ellen Dryden, wife of the sixth earl of Sanderford who at one time belonged to the diplomatic corps in Washington . . .'

There was more, typical of gossip columns in its rambling, name-dropping content but Kate was only too happy to find her name hadn't been mentioned at all. Apparently Michael Fitzgerald the third, questioned the day after the dinner, had been enigmatically silent on the subject of his companion. More like blazing angry, Kate thought cynically.

'Well, is it true?' Evidently impressed, Sally was waiting for details. 'All that about his being rich and his sister being married to an earl and his dad being a senator.'

'His father is a senator, yes. But the rest, I don't know. It might be.' Kate nodded, recalling a long ago comment Fitzgerald had made about being richer than he looked.

'He never told you?'

'Why should he? I'm just his secretary,' Kate said without thinking and grimaced. 'Correction, I *was* just his secretary.'

'You mean——' Sally's eyes widened first in astonishment and then, to Kate's horror, sheer delight as she continued, 'Well, I don't blame you. If the picture's anything to go by, he's gorgeous as well as loaded. And I suspected all the time you really liked him from how much you hated him.'

'*Sally!*' Kate broke into the other girl's raptures before they could get any more ridiculous. 'That's not what I meant! Apart from being insulting, it's the silliest thing I've ever heard considering . . .'

'Considering what?'

'We had a slight disagreement,' Kate admitted, deliberately understating it, 'and I decided to terminate my employment with him.'

But Sally, slanting her a keen look, wasn't fooled. 'Translated—he made a lunge and you told him what he could do with his job. Right?'

Kate's lips twisted. 'More or less.'

'Did you have to fight him off?' Sally quizzed.

'Not exactly.'

'*He* had to fight *you* off?'

'Sally!' exclaimed Kate but laughing despite herself, and knowing the Yorkshire girl would keep going until she heard more, she gave her a censored version of the evening's events.

'You're crazy, love,' commented Sally at the end, only half-joking. 'Why didn't you tell him your part-time lodger was your fifteen-year-old brother?'

'He didn't give me a chance,' Kate defended, not quite truthfully. 'And anyway I don't see what right he has to get mad if I *was* living with someone.'

'It's not a question of rights, love, if the man has a thing for you. Yes, I know you've told me,' Sally said as Kate was on the point of interrupting, 'but how else would you explain his behaviour.'

Kate had given it some thought since the scene two nights ago and declared cynically, 'It's obvious he's used to women falling all over him and he doesn't like it when they don't. I bet if I'd been the same, he wouldn't have given me a second glance.'

'Maybe, but I wouldn't put it to the test,' Sally advised with a dry laugh.

'I'm not likely to get the chance,' Kate sighed heavily.

Sally frowned. 'It's upset you, hasn't it? Losing the job, I mean.'

'Yes.' Kate supposed that was why her mind kept going back over the scene, regretting the bitter, hurting words they had both thrown at each other. 'I don't know if he'll give me a reference and it might be weeks before I get another job.'

'You are in a mess again, love,' Sally said sympathetically, then with some reluctance offered, 'Would you like me to check if there's anything going at the club?'

'Could you, Sally?' Kate turned hopeful eyes on her.

Sally nodded before adding as a reservation, 'The only thing is, Kate, if I recommend you to Brian Court, the manager, and you jack it in after a couple of weeks, it might be awkward for me.'

'I understand and I won't—I promise,' Kate promptly reassured. 'Even if I get another secretarial job, I can still do the club at weekends. And the extra money would mean an awful lot.'

'All right, I'll go and phone,' Sally agreed.

Kate got dressed while the other girl was upstairs. And though her stomach clenched every time she thought of working in a nightclub, she prayed there would be something available.

Sally returned smiling. 'You're in luck. One of the other weekend dealers has given in her notice so Brian jumped at the chance of hiring you. Admittedly it helped when I told him you were bright and good-looking ... and that you'd once worked in *Les Etoiles*.'

'Where?' Kate gaped.

'*Les Etoiles*—it's a nightclub in Paris,' Sally continued shamelessly. 'Really classy joint. Brian was most impressed.'

'But what if he checks with them?' Kate asked in alarm.

'Not likely. Apart from the language barrier, calling Paris isn't cheap—whereas our Brian is,' Sally confided with a grin. 'Anyway, by the time I've finished, you'll be able to deal blindfold.'

Kate doubted that very much but she let herself be carried along by the other girl's enthusiasm. First there was the matter of a suitable dress.

After a quick run through Kate's wardrobe she declared, 'Too nice, if you follow me.'

Kate didn't totally until she was whisked round the shops and made to buy three dresses. They were cheap, showy and, according to Sally, ideal for the Genevieve. Cringing at the sight of herself in silver lurex, Kate drew comfort from the assurance a couple of nights' tips would probably pay for all three.

Then it was back to the house for a four-hour practice session during which Sally taught her the finer points of 'twenty-one' as well as a whole new vocabulary of gambling terms. And by the time they had finished, Kate almost wished she could wear a blindfold so she didn't have to look at another card again in her life.

Perhaps Sally was deliberately employing shock tactics. At any rate, Kate's brain was too numb for her to be even nervous when she found herself in the Genevieve's gaming room. As Sally had said, it wasn't Monte Carlo, but neither did its tackiness reach the depths of Kate's imaginings. And though Brian Court spent the first two hours hovering, he seemed more intent on leering at her than noticing how well or otherwise, she dealt.

'You'll have to watch him—he thinks he's God's gift,' Sally warned in the taxi on the way home.

Kate just shrugged. After seven hours at the card table, she was too tired to care.

But when they parted in the hallway, she squeezed Sally's arm and smiled gratefully. 'Thanks, Sally. Thanks for everything.'

'Glad to have the company, love.' Sally smiled back and noticing Kate's bleary-eyed expression, laughed. 'I only hope you survive the weekend.'

Kate did somehow, although by the Sunday night she was so exhausted she nearly fell asleep in her last hour at the table and she slept until the afternoon on the Monday. But she still felt grateful to Sally. The tips from the Genevieve wouldn't cover Johnny's fees but she'd be able to save something towards them.

She was going upstairs to thank the Yorkshire girl again when she discovered the letter in her rack in the hallway. She frowned over the handwriting on the envelope before its familiarity struck her.

Then she went back to her flat and placing it on the table, stared at if for a full five minutes as though it was booby-trapped.

Eventually she nerved herself to rip open the envelope and take out the barely worded letter inside. Dated Friday, it read,

Dear Miss Gregory,
    Should I assume from your absence over the last two days, you wish to officially terminate your employment?

Fitzgerald

It couldn't have been simpler but Kate must have puzzled over it for half an hour. Had he expected her back? No, surely that wasn't possible. Yet his phrasing seemed to imply it. Or was it merely a request for a written resignation?

In the end she took the letter to Sally who read it once and didn't puzzle over it at all. 'An olive branch, love,' she stated confidently.

'A what?' Kate repeated in surprise.

'As in, "Come back, all is forgiven",' Sally added with a grin.

Kate's look changed to disbelief as she read the note again. 'Sally, it doesn't sound in the least bit forgiving. In fact, it doesn't even sound like Fitzgerald for that matter.'

'Exactly,' Sally replied wisely—and obscurely to Kate's mind. 'All right, he's not pleading with you but he is giving you an opening. If I were you, I'd at least go and phone him. After all, what do you have to lose?'

Her pride, Kate thought, not sharing Sally's optimism. But if there was the remotest chance of getting her job back, shouldn't she take it?

So she let Sally persuade her into calling him but its pointlessness seemed confirmed by his being out. And though Mrs O'Reilly offered to take a message, she couldn't find anything to say. She rang off, not anticipating her call to be returned, and when later that evening the young man on the second floor told her she was wanted on the telephone, she presumed it was her brother.

'Johnny,' she greeted in a pleased tone—the worst start she could have made.

'No, this is Van Fitzgerald,' a frigid voice declared at the other end of the line. 'You called me, I believe.'

'Yes. Yes, I did,' she acknowledged, then searched feverishly for something to add. The hostility in his voice was certainly no olive branch.

'Well?' he prompted as her silence threatened to stretch indefinitely.

'I received your letter and I wanted to ... to ...' she swallowed her pride and forced out, 'to say I was sorry.'

Now it was his turn to be silent for a long moment before disbelief had him echoing, 'You're sorry?'

'Yes!' Kate snapped in reflex and if she regretted her sharpness, it obviously helped Fitzgerald regain his balance.

'May I ask what you're sorry for, Miss Gregory?' he asked with a drawling sarcasm that had Kate gritting her teeth.

What *was* she sorry for? She picked the only thing for which she could genuinely apologise. 'I shouldn't have said your book was bloody stupid. It's not,' she offered tentatively.

'You can't imagine how relieved I am to hear that, Miss Gregory,' he replied even more sarcastically. 'Was there anything else? Or did you just phone to deliver that book review?'

The temptation to slam the receiver down was almost irresistible. She had to be wasting her time. She wasn't even sure whether she was trying to get her job back or absolving her conscience for losing it.

'I was wondering——' she began promisingly enough, but found she just couldn't humiliate herself any more. She changed to muttering, 'Never mind, it doesn't matter.'

'Don't hang up yet!' He forestalled her intention with an unexpected force that made Kate jump. Then after another lengthy pause, he resumed in a much quieter tone, 'After all, you never know—ask and you just may receive.'

Stunned for a moment, Kate managed to overcome both suspicion and pride to choke out, 'Could I possibly withdraw my resignation, Mr Fitzgerald?'

She was left holding her breath for a suffocatingly long time before he muttered, 'I'll see you tomorrow,' and abruptly rang off.

She turned up early the next day, with little idea why he'd given her a second chance and dreading their first meeting. She was relieved when Mrs O'Reilly announced he wasn't yet up.

'Working late again,' she informed Kate as she pressed a cup of coffee on her. 'Not that he's had much success the last few days if the waste paper bins are anything to go by. And as surly as a tinker's dog.'

'Really,' commented Kate, feeling a little sick at this colourful description of Fitzgerald's mood.

'Sure, it's glad I am that you're back, dear,' smiled Mrs O'Reilly, 'for I'm thinking you'll be sorting him out.'

Uncertain what 'sorting out' entailed, Kate didn't share the Irish woman's confidence. 'I'm afraid I've had very little experience of tinkers' dogs, Mrs O,' she joked weakly. 'And to be honest, we had a bit of an argument last week.'

'Ah well, that's to be expected with his temper and all,' said Mrs O'Reilly as though it was another of his admirable qualities. 'A black Irish temper he has—just like my husband Liam.'

Kate had heard about Mrs O'Reilly's late husband before and knowing the other enjoyed talking of him, she asked, 'And how did you sort *him* out, Mrs O?'

'Oh, a woman has ways, dearie, a woman has ways,' Mrs O'Reilly replied with a leery smile that made Kate laugh.

It was at that point, a third voice cut into the conversation, 'When you've quite finished, Miss Gregory, perhaps you wouldn't mind catching up on your backlog of work.'

Both women turned to find their employer, still dressed in towelling robe, watching them from the doorway. Mrs O'Reilly gave Kate a 'told-you-so' look but, yet to acclimatise herself to the change in atmosphere, Kate gasped at the criticism. How many times had he himself told her not to work through her lunch, to take coffee breaks whenever she wanted?

'Did you wish to say something, Miss Gregory?' he demanded at her open-mouthed expression.

Kate most definitely did but by some miracle, she restrained the impulse, and he departed after a last imperious glance.

She pulled a face at his retreating back and commented sourly, 'I think you're being hard on the dog, Mrs O.'

The Irish woman chuckled and as Kate rose to go, warned humorously, 'Sure that's him in a good mood, Katie girl.'

Kate hoped she was joking but very quickly discovered she wasn't. Black temper was a fair description of Fitzgerald's mood throughout that week. For nothing she did was right any more. She'd been in the habit of guessing at the more indecipherable of his writing : now she was informed, highly sarcastically, that she should refrain from any 'creative urges' she might have and confine herself to typing what he'd written.

But, by following his instructions and consulting him on every doubtful word, she pleased him even less. And she could only fume in silence when he suggested she try using her initiative for a change.

Worse, she appeared to have lost any immunity to him. It wasn't just the restraint it took not to retaliate but the unnerving fact that she couldn't seem to prevent it getting to her.

By Friday it was a close run thing which broke first—Fitzgerald's temper or her nerve. In the morning Kate had tentatively asked if she might rearrange her hours so she started later on Mondays; and when he demanded the reason, she couldn't come up with one quickly enough before he walked off, leaving the question unanswered. She assumed that meant 'no' and could only hope after working at the Genevieve till the early hours, she did not sleep in.

Then late afternoon, just as she was tidying her desk, he reappeared with a letter from the French professor, requiring translation. Normally he allowed her to study the professor's letters beforehand but this time she had barely drawn it from the envelope when he barked at her, 'Well, what does it say?'

Kate's French was fairly fluent on an everyday conversation level but after the opening pleasantries, the subject matter became more complex. Without Fitzgerald scowling every time she faltered, she might have managed the lengthy dissertation. But with each sentence her translation deteriorated until she began to go blank on even the most common words and finally, after yet another sarcastic interruption, she found herself humiliatingly close to tears.

'I'm sorry—I can't do it,' she choked out, and rose to gather her belongings, intent on escaping before she broke down completely.

But he caught her by the arm and though she bent her head, he saw the glisten of tears on her dark lashes. 'Kate, are you all right?'

'Yes.' A sob muffled her voice. 'Please, Van, just let me go.'

'You'll come back—on Monday, I mean?' The

enquiry sounded surprisingly anxious and he added, 'Whatever time you like.'

Confused by the sudden change in him, Kate raised her head to discover a stark expression on his face. Warily she nodded but the moment he released her, she again made for the door.

And though he murmured after her, 'It'll be different, Kate, you'll see,' she did not turn.

If she had, he would have seen the fear and distrust in her eyes.

CHAPTER NINE

BUT if Kate still had reservations when she reported for work late on the Monday, his very casualness soon dispelled them.

Gone was the scowling, brooding tyrant of a boss; back was the smiling, genial American; and though she rejected Mrs O's credit for the transformation, she couldn't help agreeing, however cynically, that Fitzgerald could be a 'lovely man' when he tried.

In fact, by the middle of the next week when Johnny came home for half-term she didn't have to pretend enthusiasm for the job. Nor was it too much of an effort to concentrate on Van Fitzgerald's better qualities at Johnny's request for a rundown on her new employer.

But perhaps she went a bit overboard because when she told a delighted Johnny she had a date all three nights of the weekend—rather than explain about the Genevieve—her brother immediately jumped to the conclusion it was with the American himself.

Of course later, it was to seem very foolish not to have disillusioned him, but on the spur of the moment it appeared a lot easier to let him go on thinking it. Otherwise she would have had to invent another man, important enough to monopolise her weekend. So, yes, at the time, it had been the line of least resistance—an apparently harmless lie that pleased him and saved her telling more. Or did until one day about four weeks later.

A bitterly cold Friday it was, at the end of November, and if the weather wasn't sufficient to depress the spirits, a one-day stoppage by London Transport was. Kate arrived at work, blue with the cold, and already worrying how quickly she could walk home again to have a bath before her evening's work at the Genevieve.

Mrs O'Reilly, however, thawed her out with hot tea and she spent a lazy morning, checking she had done all the work Fitzgerald had left. He was away for three days in Paris, meeting with the professor, and he wasn't expected back till the evening.

Instead he turned up while the two women were lunching in the kitchen, Kate having long since been persuaded to take her meal with the others. She did a doubletake when she glanced up from her meal to see him framed in the doorway, looking unfamiliar yet undeniably handsome in white silk shirt and grey suit. And perhaps caught off-guard by his appearance, she experienced the most curious rush of pleasure that he'd come back early.

Naturally she tried not to show it but she felt a blush hit her cheeks when he smiled, his eyes lazily appraising as he made no attempt to hide his pleasure in seeing her again.

Then Mrs O'Reilly noticed him with a cheery, 'Sure it's yourself, Mr Van. And how was gay Paree?'

'Not half as gay as it's given credit for, Mrs O.,' he chuckled wryly, pushing away from the door to sit down with them. 'And how's everything here?'

The question was directed at Kate and she replied succinctly, 'Fine.'

Mrs O'Reilly was more expansive. 'Well, apart from the weather. Frozen Kate was this morning when she arrived, what with the strike—bus *and* underground this time. You were lucky you left your car at Heathrow.'

'Yes,' he nodded, 'although I've been stuck in a traffic queue from there.'

'So you won't have had dinner,' Mrs O'Reilly announced, immediately rising to go to the stove. 'Steak and kidney pud—I cooked for three just in case.'

While Mrs O'Reilly dished up, Kate took the chance to escape, muttering about some fictitious work she had yet to do. Much to her discomfort, she was discovered staring idly out of the window when he appeared in the study mid-afternoon.

But he simply smiled and suggested in his easy-going way, 'You might as well call it a day if you've finished. I'll give you a lift home.'

Tempted, Kate wondered if Mrs O'Reilly had press-ganged him into offering. 'Are you sure? The traffic might still be jammed up.'

He shrugged. 'I'm not really in the mood to work and I've nothing else planned.'

Remembering the unpleasantness of her walk to work, Kate made no further attempt to talk him out of it. The roads were busy but he didn't seem to mind. While he edged through Kensington High Street, he told her some amusing stories about his visit to the Sorbonne. Apparently the professor had turned out to be slightly eccentric and although claiming to speak English, it had been hard going to understand him.

'You should have come,' Van said, watching her as she laughed unguardedly at one of the worst muddles the language barrier had created. 'You would have enjoyed it.'

'Yes, perhaps,' Kate conceded with a smile. 'He sounds quite a character.'

'He was.' Van chuckled and then lapsed into silence for a few moments before adding, 'And I certainly would have enjoyed it more, Kate, if you'd been there.'

Kate glanced at him, confirming the impression of seriousness she'd heard in his voice. She sensed he was waiting for her to say something. She couldn't.

Over a month had elapsed since their last quarrel and against all the odds, they did have a sort of friendship. They worked well together, talked about neutral subjects and at times shared a joke. But once in a while he would make some comment which, in Kate's view,

threatened their fragile peace. Sometimes it angered her
that he did, seeing only careless charm behind the
words, and she never responded. Today she felt
inexplicably guilty as she turned her head to stare out of
the window.

They seemed to take an age, a now oppressively silent
age, to reach Notting Hill Gate and Kate was on the
point of suggesting he drop her off on the main road
when she spotted Sally, struggling home with two
shopping bags.

'That's the girl who lives in the flat above me,' she
told him as they drew almost level with Sally. 'Could we
possibly stop and give her a lift?'

'Sure.' He pulled into the side of the road while Kate
rolled down her window to hail Sally.

When the other girl was installed in the back seat,
Kate made some hasty introductions, automatically
referring to him as Mr Fitzgerald.

Swivelling round to offer his hand, he dismissed her
formality with, 'Nice to meet you, and it's Van.'

'Yes, Kate's mentioned you,' Sally said, her tone
guileless. 'And we've spoken on the phone.'

'Have we? Ah yes, I remember,' he acknowledged
after a second's thought. 'Then perhaps I should
apologise for making you the bearer of bad tidings on
that particular occasion,' he drawled with an amused
smile.

Sally grinned back. 'That's okay. And thanks for
stopping.'

'My pleasure,' he said, smile widening appreciatively
on Sally for a moment before he turned back in his seat.
Flattery will get you everywhere, Kate thought a trifle
sourly, as she recognised the effect he'd had on Sally.

Indeed the Northern girl gave Kate a quizzical look
that questioned if this was the same American she had
described at various times as brash, arrogant and
impossible. Obviously Sally didn't find him so, and she
chatted with Van for the rest of the route back.

By the time they reached the house, Kate was
conscious of a distinct lack of grace on her part. Not
only had he allowed her to leave work a couple of hours

early, but he'd saved her a cold walk home. So it seemed a matter of good manners to offer him a cup of coffee this time. Nevertheless she first checked that Sally wanted one before she extended the invitation elsewhere. From his half-mocking smile, the fact of it was not lost on him.

Kate was relieved to find the flat relatively tidy. She went through to the kitchen alcove and quickly made up a tray of coffee and biscuits, hoping Sally didn't feel too awkward left on her own with the American. When she returned to the living room, however, they were already engaged in a conversation about Sally's modelling career.

And while Sally chatted away with her usual liveliness, Van was at his charming, good-humoured best. For two people who had very little in common, they got on like a house on fire. It took Kate about quarter of an hour to start resenting it, and another quarter to admit it to herself.

Exactly what she resented she hadn't quite worked out but when Sally began to make reluctant leaving noises she made no effort to detain her.

In fact she was almost hustling Sally to the door when the other girl turned and clapped a hand on her forehead. 'Oh damn, I forgot to tell you. Johnny phoned earlier. He's coming home for the weekend.'

'Coming home?' Kate echoed.

'Yes, he didn't have much time before the pips went but he said for you not to worry.'

Kate instantly began to worry. The school did not encourage the boys to come home during termtime.

'Did he say what time to expect him?'

'About four he reckoned, but he's probably having problems getting across London because of the strike.' Sally observed Kate's troubled expression. 'You don't think anything bad's happened to him, do you?'

Kate shook her head, realising Sally was thinking along the lines of expulsion.

'Tell us later then,' Sally added, reminding her of their evening at the club—and then of their audience as she glanced past her. 'Bye, Van. Perhaps I'll see you again.'

'Count on it,' he drawled back. 'And till then, good luck with the modelling.'

'Thanks, I need it,' Sally laughed back.

'Not from where I'm standing,' denied Van gallantly, his eyes complimenting Sally's tall, well-proportioned figure.

'Who said Americans have no charm?' she asked of no one in particular but her smile slipped slightly when she caught Kate's glare and remembered who *had* actually said it to her.

As astute as ever, Van quipped, 'I can guess—but I wouldn't believe everything you hear.'

'Oh, I don't. Seeing's believing, as they say,' Sally returned, and in support of the cliché, gave the American a look that seemed to approve every lean, muscular inch of him.

Unable to stand much more of this mutual appreciation society, Kate cut in, 'Aren't you in a hurry, Sally?'

The Northern girl registered her sharp tone with the slight lift of her eyebrows but didn't seem to take exception to it, her smile wry as she returned, 'Yes, right you are. I'll leave you to it then.'

The moment the door closed, Kate regretted her almost indecent haste to be rid of Sally.

'Nice girl,' Van comented succinctly but his lazy-eyed smile suggested he was referring to more than Sally's personality.

'Well, don't worry, I'm sure your appreciation was noted!' Kate snapped impulsively.

'What's that supposed to mean?' he asked with an infuriating expression of innocence.

'Like your interest in Sally,' she retorted, 'I would have thought it too obvious for words.'

'My interest in Sally,' he echoed, shedding his genial manner, '*if* it exists outside your imagination, Miss Gregory, is surely *my* business . . . *isn't it?*'

Somewhere between embarrassment and fury, Kate was stuck for a suitable reply. He was right—it was none of her business. Finally she took refuge in picking up the coffee things, only to have him follow her through to the kitchen alcove.

'You haven't answered my question yet.'

'Haven't I? I'm afraid I've forgotten it.'

'Do you want me to repeat it?'

'No!'

Kate banged the biscuit tin back on a shelf.

'Why are you so angry?' he asked and not giving her the chance to deny it, speculated, 'You know, if I didn't know better I would say you were jealous.'

'*Jealous!*' Kate turned on him furiously. 'That has to be *the* most ridiculous thing you've ever said.'

'Has it?' he jibed.

'Yes, it damn well has!' she flared back.

'Then why are you yelling?' he challenged.

'*I am not* . . . yelling!' Kate almost shouted, and then at the sheer mockery in his eyes, bit out, 'If you don't mind, I think you'd better go,' making it plain she wasn't offering him a choice by brushing past him. But she never reached the door far less completed her intention of holding it open for him.

He caught her up just inside the main living room and spun her round. Not expecting it, Kate nearly lashed out at him and if she controlled the impulse, her quick rise to panic was revealed in her eyes.

'Hey, I only want to talk to you.' Van released his grip on her arm and gave her a searching look. 'There's no reason to be scared.'

'Don't be silly!' She desperately tried to cover that instinctive nervousness. 'I'm not scared. Why should I be?'

'I don't know—you tell me.' He glanced briefly at her mouth, making Kate aware she was biting her lower lip. 'Perhaps you're worried that your *friend* won't like my being here.'

'Friend?' Kate frowned.

'Johnny, isn't it?' he prompted curtly.

'Yes,' Kate confirmed, just as curtly.

'I've always wondered why you said yes in the park when I asked if you were meeting your *John*. You must have found my ignorance quite amusing.'

The hard note in his voice told Kate her supposed

amusement wasn't shared but carelessly she agreed, 'Hilarious.'

'Then it is the same man—the one you live with?' he rasped back, and at her nod, derided, 'He didn't look much more than a boy to me.'

'He's older than he looks,' she lied shamelessly.

'He'd have to be,' Van muttered, his lips twisting.

Provoked, Kate couldn't stop herself challenging, 'And what's *that* supposed to mean?'

'Come on, Kate—you may try to give the impression of being one hundred percent ice,' he mocked her cold stare and without warning, curled long fingers round the nape of her neck, almost playfully stroking the soft skin, 'but there are times . . . like that day in the park, remember? When you responded, and there and then I wanted to——'

'You *made* me!' Kate cut in angrily.

'And you hated every minute, didn't you?' he returned, a mocking smile suggesting the opposite.

'Yes!' she ground out.

'Little liar,' he taunted under his breath.

'I suppose your conceited male ego——' Kate began scathingly before an arm suddenly clasped her waist and she changed to gasping, 'What are you doing?'

'Satisfying a point to my conceited male ego,' he drawled and backed her against the nearest wall to contain her struggling. 'Calm down, will you? Just a kiss—nothing more. And you can always console yourself with the fact I'm *making* you.'

With an explosive sigh of frustration, Kate gave up trying to twist out of his arms—it was obviously hurting her a lot more than it was him—but she spat back, 'I know your *just a kiss*, Van Fitzgerald!'

'Good—because it's been so long I was worried you'd forgotten . . . and I'm damned if I can,' he said, his voice lowering to a soft murmur.

The mockery had gone from his eyes, and Kate felt her own anger slipping away. Vulnerable without it, she started to turn her head aside but a hand caught her chin, forcing her to return his disturbingly intense gaze.

'Why do you do that, Kate? Why do you always look away when I try to tell you . . .' His words faded as Kate lifted her head fractionally to stem their disarming flow and he took the unconscious invitation with a deep, satisfied groan.

Kate shuddered at the touch of his lips: lips that first merely brushed against hers, without demand yet arousing, gently nibbling at her mouth, gradually parting it—then suddenly, when every sense was lulled, invading with a total intimacy.

Startled, she tried to draw away but the hand tangled in her hair forced her to stay still, to accept the now hungry, probing kiss, filling her mouth so she could scarcely breathe, shocking her into awareness of his desire, taking what he wanted while the hard length of his body trapped her helplessly against the wall.

Yet when he eventually dragged his mouth away she did not scream or struggle, did not prevent the fingers pushing aside her blouse.

She simply clung to his shoulders as he bent to kiss, then tenderly bite the skin at her throat, breathing her name over and over until she raised a hand to tentatively caress the back of his neck, turned her face to rest her lips almost shyly on his brow.

But when he responded with a low, husky mumur, she felt an urge to please him more. To thread her fingers into the thickness of his hair, to brush her lips, warm and moist, against the muscle beating at his temple, then trail them across his hard cheekbone as his head began to rise until their mouths met once more and opened to the other on a sweet moan of need and desire.

And Kate thought, 'Just a kiss'—a last weak caution to herself before she gave up thinking at all—and there was only the moment and the man and the heady feeling he aroused with his hard persuasive mouth.For if she tensed when a hand slipped inside her unbuttoned blouse, it was not fear that had her pulses beating wildly as his fingers spread against the swell of her breast and slowly began to circle the already hardened peak. Infinitely slowly while she gasped with the pleasure of it and her soft cries of desire could be heard beneath the sound of his own ragged breathing.

He lifted his mouth from hers and perhaps it was a measure of how dazed Kate was that she didn't resent the satisfaction in his smile.

'Kate. . . .' His hands came up to frame her face and for endless moments he simply stared at her, as though that was enough. But when he spoke again, it was to murmur, 'Kate, let me show you how I feel . . . completely show you.'

'Van, I——' Her voice caught in her throat.

'Please, Kate,' he urged, no arrogance in the plea, almost anguish in his eyes at the doubt in hers. 'I realise you don't feel the same. But you feel something, don't you?'

'Yes . . . no . . . I'm not sure . . .' she stammered in quick succession, her strongest feeling confusion. 'I shouldn't have . . .'

She shook her head as she thought of the things she shouldn't have done, shouldn't have let him do. A sense of shame returned, made her fingers fly to her blouse but he was quicker, a hand closing on her wrist to stop her buttoning it.

'Why not, Kate?' he asked, still a curious tenderness in his gaze.

Eyes caught by his, Kate groped for the answer, feeling it should be obvious but discovering it no longer was. Not even the fears of inexperience seemed enough to make her keep pushing Van away any more. But she had to, hadn't she?

Van watched her withdrawing from him and urged, 'Kate?'

'I can't—won't get involved with you,' she forced out.

'Why not?' he repeated raggedly. 'I wouldn't hurt you, Kate. I couldn't the way I——'

'That's not it,' she broke in, knowing she shouldn't listen to any persuasion, admit to any weakness. Out of desperation she resorted to saying, 'You seem to have forgotten I have other . . . commitments.'

The flicker of anger crossing his face suggested he had—or at least considered it an irrelevancy now.

'Maybe, but you seem to find them relatively easy to forget too,' he reminded her, eyes sliding to her half-opened blouse. When she again made to do it up with her free hand, he captured it as well and holding them both in front of him, the determination in his voice hardened. 'Not one single ring, Kate. That's no commitment, and if the guy's crazy enough to treat you like dirt—'

'He doesn't!' Kate defended automatically.

'No? Be honest, Kate,' he appealed, his brows drawing into a heavy frown at her stubbornness, 'I may not pay you a fortune but you can surely afford a better place to live than this. So where does the money go, huh? And you hated having to crawl back to me for your job, but something made you, didn't it? Or someone?'

Kate stared back in astonishment, both at his interpretation of things and the concern etched deeply in the strong lines of his face.

She shook her head. 'You don't understand.'

'Then explain it to me,' he urged.

'I can't—it's too ...' she trailed off and guiltily lowered her eyes from the anxiety in his.

But he saw the gesture differently, releasing her hands to place his own on her shoulders. 'Don't be frightened, Kate, I can protect you from him—whatever hold he has on you,' he promised thickly as he drew her forward till her forehead rested against his chest, and when Kate trembled at his closeness, he went on, 'Whether you want me or not, I'll look after you, Kate. No strings, I swear it. You could come and——'

'Please, Van!' Kate implored him not to say more before she could tell him she neither needed nor deserved his protection.

He seemed to understand for he fell silent but she still floundered for the right words to reveal her true situation. And when a hand lifted to gently cradle her head, she found herself returning the quiet embrace, wanting to hold on to the warmth and strength he offered for just a moment longer.

A moment too long ...

*   *   *

She couldn't really blame Van for what followed. When he felt her arms steal round him, he drew her closer and turned his face into her hair, seemingly unconscious of anything but Kate as he whispered her name like a caress.

Kate herself only barely registered the faint scratching of a key turning a lock. But when she looked past Van's shoulder and completely over-reacted to her brother's sudden appearance in the doorway, she certainly couldn't blame him either for misunderstanding her desperate struggle to be free of Van's embrace.

One moment Johnny was rooted to the spot, the next leaping for the American as he released Kate and began to wheel round. Luckily, perhaps, there was no stand-up fight for her brother caught him still turning and off-balance, and they both went crashing to the floor, knocking over the coffee table on the way down. Johnny landed on top but that advantage didn't last for long as a much stronger Fitzgerald rolled him easily on to his back, to trap him against the floor. Then he raised his fist . . .

And Kate broke out of her dumb shock, screaming, 'Van, for God's sake, don't! Please don't!'

Her appeal was unnecessary. Van was already frozen in mid-action, staring in disbelief at the boyish face beneath him.

'He's my brother, my younger brother—he's only fifteen!' A hovering Kate garbled out although she sensed he was no longer going to hit the boy.

Indeed it was Johnny who took a wild swipe in the breathing space offered and was restrained from taking another as his arms were pinned on either side of his body.

'Easy, kid,' Van muttered, slowly shifting some of his weight from the boy. 'I wasn't hurting your . . . sister. Tell him, Kate!' he ordered when the fierce light in Johnny's eyes remained.

'Yes, Johnny, he wasn't——' she began hastily but faltered when her brother's gaze, now on her, made her aware once more of her gaping blouse. Colouring heatedly and fumbling with the buttons, she rushed on, 'This is Van—Van Fitzgerald, the American I told you about. He was . . .we were . . .' then trailed off, realising it might be fairly obvious what he'd interrupted.

Apparently it was. Johnny looked from Kate to the man above him, laid his head back on the floor with a thump and shutting his eyes, groaned aloud, 'Oh, hell's bells!' in almost comic self-reproach.

At any length it seemed to amuse Fitzgerald as mouth slanting, he pushed himself up from the floor. Kate, however, who had never heard her brother swear before, couldn't help a frown of disapproval as she knelt down beside him.

Opening his eyes again, Johnny caught it and mumbled, 'I'm sorry, Kate, I behaved like a total idiot.'

'No, it was my fault,' she declared, cringing when she recalled her own stupid reaction. 'Are you all right?'

'Yes, sure.' He grinned to prove it.

'Here.' Van bent down to help the boy to his feet and offered his hand. 'A little late for formalities, maybe, but pleased to meet you all the same . . . Johnny.'

'You too, Mr Fitzgerald.' The boy returned the handshake politely.

'Van,' the American insisted before sitting down with a slight grimace. Kate wondered if he'd hurt his bad leg but was too unnerved to ask.

There was a moment's silence and then Johnny joined him on the sofa. 'Look Mr—Van, I'm awfully sorry about the way I acted—attacking you and all.'

Fitzgerald smiled, dismissing, 'Forget it. No damage done. And I can understand your wanting to protect your sister . . . Believe me, I can.'

'Well, yes,' Johnny went on gravely, 'but I don't want you to think I'm going to be in the way or anything. I mean Kate's told me you're going out together as well as being her boss and I'd just like to say that . . . that I . . .' Johnny finally ran out off steam, inhibited by the American's lack of response other than blank bewilderment.

But far too late for Kate's comfort. She gave up on any hope of rescuing the situation and sank down in the armchair, to wait for Fitzgerald to deduce he wasn't the only one she'd deceived. It didn't take him long as his eyes locked with hers and their appraising stare made her dread what he might say next.

The last thing she expected was for him to put Johnny at his ease by replying, 'I hope you were going to say that you approve.'

'Rather,' the boy declared earnestly, unconscious of any wryness in the remark. 'Kate's told me all about you being a war reporter. I bet that's awfully exciting.'

'At times.' Van shrugged.

'And dangerous?' Johnny added with evident fascination and Kate sensed the American was about to be bombarded with questions.

'Johnny—what are you doing home? Has something happened at school?' she said, distracting him.

'Food poisoning,' he replied succinctly but when Kate looked alarmed, quickly explained, 'Oh, I haven't got it. Just one or two of the boys so they wanted those of us who could, to go home for the weekend while they traced the cause.'

'You're at boarding school?' inserted Van.

'Yes, in Suffolk,' Johnny supplied before the question struck him as odd. 'Didn't Kate tell you?'

'To be honest, no,' Van admitted, 'she's been a bit *reticent* about some things. And I guess I imagined you to be slightly older.'

As a version of the truth, it was probably the most favourable to Kate. She supposed she should have been grateful. But she felt more nervous, wondering why he was behaving so damn reasonably.

Particularly when he went on, 'Anyway, now we've met, you can fill me in with the details she's missed. In fact,' he consulted the gold watch on his wrist, 'how about us all going out for a bite to eat? It's still early but we should be able to get something—a hamburger or pizza, whatever you prefer ...'

'Hamburger,' Johnny accepted readily.

But his enthusiasm was immediately overriden by Kate muttering, 'I'm afraid I can't this evening.'

Van didn't seem too surprised by her reply but if he

thought it a flat refusal, he had no need to challenge it.
He just sat back and let Johnny do it for him.

'Why not?' her brother pursued.

'I've made other arrangements,' she returned evas-
ively.

'Arrangements?' Her vagueness was quizzed.

'I have a date,' she said after a vain search for a
different excuse.

'A date.' Her brother's eyes switched from her to Van
and back again. 'With someone else?' he blurted out
less than tactfully.

'I—yes,' Kate decided not to elaborate on it, praying
Johnny would leave it at that.

Doubtful, if Van hadn't suddenly cut in with, 'Looks
like we're not the only two fish in the sea, Johnny.'

What is he playing at? Kate asked herself after a
probing glance discerned absolutely nothing from his
bland expression.

'But I thought you and Kate——' Johnny began
again, only this time caught himself up, and finished by
mumbling, 'I seem to have got things wrong.'

'Not entirely,' Van reassured, his eyes on Kate, 'Let's
just say I'm working on it.'

What was Johnny going to make of that? Kate
wondered, giving the American an exasperated look.
Come to that, what did she make of it?

'Meanwhile,' he added, slanting a smile at the boy,
'why don't you and I go out for that hamburger, okay?'

'If you like,' Johnny agreed, shyer now Kate wasn't
included.

'And we could catch a movie afterwards, perhaps,'
Van continued.

'Have you seen *Galactic Seven*?' Johnny's enthusiasm
was rekindled.

Van shook his head, obviously quite prepared to put
up with anything the boy chose. Suspecting she was
being malicious, Kate couldn't help hoping that
Johnny's adolescent taste bored the American silly.

In fact if she could have, she would have objected to
the entire outing. But on what grounds?

In any case, Fitzgerald was in one of his unstoppable

moods. They'd left before it even occurred to her she should warn Johnny to be discreet. As she changed hurriedly, she could only reassure herself that Johnny rarely referred to their old life nowadays.

On the way to the club, Sally brought the American into conversation but was soon discouraged by a lack of response. Kate no longer felt able to discuss him in the same clearcut terms she had used before, and she certainly didn't want to dwell on the afternoon's events.

Yet despite an exhausting evening, later she lay in bed sleepless, remembering both his words and the concern mirrored by deep blue eyes—that unfinished promise of no strings if she came and . . . lived with him? Was that what he had been about to say?

It should have seemed an impossible idea, as impossible as working for him had once seemed. Only it didn't when images of Van filled her mind. Untidy, casual, at times infuriating—but so clever and amusing and loving too.

No, not *loving*—that was illusion. Desire tempered by tenderness; passion that wanted to give pleasure as well as take. But not real loving.

Too little to risk loving him back, she thought, still believing the choice was hers to make.

CHAPTER TEN

THE next morning Johnny was in high spirits. At first Kate was relieved that he was more intent on talking of his evening than asking about hers.

That was until she realised Johnny had a bad case of hero-worship. In all fairness she doubted the influence was deliberate. Experience told her it would have been more a matter of Van shrugging casual replies about his work as a correspondent to her little brother's relentless questioning.

And it appeared the liking was mutual. Subject to her

approval, the American had invited Johnny out again.
This time to a basketball game and even Kate had heard
of the Harlem Globetrotters, famous for their blend of
skill and humour. She hadn't the heart to tell her
brother he couldn't go. Indeed, when she thought of her
evening ahead at the Genevieve, she was surprised into
envying Johnny's. A disconcerting feeling she tried to
shake off.

But on the Sunday it still lingered as Johnny
chattered on about his outing until it was disturbingly
like the resentment she'd felt with Sally two days
earlier.

'What's wrong? And don't say "nothing",' Johnny
forestalled when he couldn't fail to notice her apparent
lack of interest. 'You don't want me to talk about Van,
do you?'

Was she that transparent? Kate thought as she
evaded, 'I'd sooner hear how school's going. It'll be
your "O" level prelims next week, won't it?'

'Yes, and I've been working really hard for them, I
promise,' he disposed of her distraction before
persisting, 'Why don't you like him any more, Kate? I
think he's super.'

'So I noticed,' she remarked, tone dry.

'*Seriously*, Kate,' he reproached.

'All right—I do like him, Johnny. I just don't want
to . . .'

Kate broke off, on the point of saying she just didn't
want to like him *too much*. Would Johnny understand
that?

Johnny saw it in simpler terms. 'Is it the other fellow
you're going out with? Do you like him better?'

'Maybe,' Kate replied, telling herself 'maybe' wasn't
an outright lie.

'But last time I was home you were keen on Van—
and that was only a month ago.'

'Yes, I know but . . . but I met this other man since
then.'

'What's his name?'

'Name?' Kate's mind went completely blank for a
second.

'And where *did* you meet him?' he pursued, almost as though he knew she was lying.

She dismissed the idea as she stated firmly, 'Look, Johnny, he's not important either. A casual friendship, no more.'

'But you go out with him *all* the time,' Johnny pointed out with boyish emphasis. '*And* you don't come home till awfully late. Last night it was past four.'

Gradually cornered, Kate found herself snapping, 'When I come in is my business, Johnny, and I don't need you checking up on me. So let's drop the subject!'

The sharp reprimand silenced him for a long moment and brought a flush of colour to his face. 'I wasn't checking up, Kate,' he eventually mumbled, his tone very subdued, 'I woke up when you snipped the door. And I know I'm too young to tell you what to do. I just worry about you because . . . well, we have to look after each other now, don't we?'

'Oh, Johnny, I'm sorry.' Kate sighed over her own lack of understanding and crossed to give him a quick hug. 'Of course we do. But there's no reason to worry.'

'Honestly, Kate?' He looked straight at her.

It was that earnest 'honestly' which did it—suddenly filled eyes, tired from the strain of working too many hours, with tears. She glanced away. 'Please, Johnny, everything's fine.'

Then she rose quickly on the pretext of making a cup of coffee, hoping he hadn't seen that moment's weakness. But he was quiet for the rest of the afternoon, and even quieter when they parted next morning.

She went in to work at midday as usual on Monday—and as usual Van proved to be totally unpredictable. Expecting questions or accusations, she was completely thrown by his casual manner. One personal remark he directed at her, asking whether Johnny had gone back to school, and shrugged aside her awkward thanks for entertaining her brother.

Other than that, it was as if the events of Friday had never happened. Kate puzzled over his behaviour until she eventually figured out what it must mean. On reflection it seemed obvious: he had lost interest in her—that was all there was to it.

And stubbornly she refused to admit there was anything but tiredness in the dejection she felt the whole week long.

Certainly the weeks of holding down two jobs were beginning to tell on Kate. In some ways the Genevieve was more exhausting than her secretarial duties for the sheer monotony of playing 'twenty-one' hour after hour, made concentration a monumental effort.

That weekend was particularly bad for she no longer had Sally for moral support. The previous Wednesday the other girl had landed her first major modelling assignment and had promptly given up her work at the club. Since then Brian Court, the manager, had been especially obnoxious to her as Sally's friend—though Kate suspected her past refusals to have a drink with him in his flat upstairs, also contributed to his vindictive behaviour.

Aware of the strain she was under, Sally had tried to persuade her to leave the Genevieve at the same time and Kate had been tempted. With her next month's pay cheque, she could just afford Johnny's fees for the following term. But the thought of Christmas had stopped her. She wanted to compensate for the flat's dreary atmosphere with the one present guaranteed to make Johnny blissfully oblivious—a microcomputer.

So somehow she found the stamina to keep going. By that Sunday, however, she felt drained and when one of the club's regulars, Bernie Leyton, appeared at her table, her spirits sunk further.

Rumour had it that he was a boxing promoter and the two 'heavies' who constantly hovered round him, positively looked like ex-fighters with their battered faces and brawny frames. And Leyton himself was, to put it mildly, an odd customer.

It wasn't a case of what he said—more what he didn't. He signalled whether he wanted a card or not. Win or lose, he made no comment. And when he needed another drink, he simply pushed his glass aside and one of his 'heavies' jumped to fetch a refill from the casino bar.

Still, she could have tolerated his silence. It was his glassy-eyed stare that really disturbed her; practically every time she glanced up from the table, his eyes seemed to be on her rather than the cards. Difficult to ignore while he remained her sole customer, flanked by his two pugnacious companions, it came as an immense relief when the fourth chair was suddenly occupied. She looked up from the table with an automatic smile for her new customer.

It died, however, from the shock of recognition when she met all too familiar blue eyes. For an instant she was dazed enough to believe it coincidence—one awful coincidence like that time in the park. But there was no surprise in Van Fitzgerald's expression, only contempt.

She froze in the middle of dealing the next hand until a rasping voice asked, 'Something wrong?'

Then she switched her startled gaze to Bernie Leyton, almost as shocked that he had actually spoken. With a slight shake of her head, she gathered her wits together and resumed the deal in the belief Van would hardly create a scene in public.

'*Card*, sir,' she repeated when he neither signalled nor spoke but maintained an unnerving stare, if anything worse than Bernie Leyton's.

Damn him, Kate thought, her discomfort changing to anger. 'Please, Van,'—a request for him to either play or leave.

He did neither, demanding instead, 'What the hell are you doing in this joint, Kate?'

His derisive tone made Kate glare back at him in speechless exasperation. And when Bernie Leyton again spoke, this time to ask, 'Is this man bothering you?' she was half tempted to say yes. At any rate she toyed briefly with the idea before she noticed his two henchmen tense up.

'No!' she exclaimed hastily. 'No, he's—he's about to leave. Aren't you?' she added pointedly to Van. Only he missed the point altogether. If he gave the other gamblers a cursory glance, it was clearly dismissive as he turned back to her, 'No—not unless you come with me.'

'*Van,*' she said through gritted teeth, '*please go away.*'

'Not without you,' he replied with a single-minded obstinacy.

Once more Bernie Leyton chimed in, 'I think you are bothering the lady, mister, and I don't like it. And what's more, neither do my boys.'

But Van seemed insensible to the threat in the rasping undertone, muttering, 'In that case I suggest you and your boys go to another table—this one's closing,' before he stood up to reach an arm out towards Kate. There was nothing aggressive in the gesture but it was never completed.

Kate watched in horror as one of Leyton's *boys* swung Van round, and while the other quickly pinned his arms, delivered a rapid succession of brutal punches to the ribs before flooring him with a blow on the jaw. By the time most people in the gaming room had noticed the disruption, it was over.

A neat professional job that had Kate initially too stunned to move. But when she observed that Van was not only still quite remarkably conscious he was actually contemplating getting to his feet for round two, she was on the floor in seconds, restraining him.

'For God's sake, don't get up!' she hissed.

Shaking his head to clear it, he tested his jaw for breakage. 'Brother, who are those guys?'

'Bethnal Green's answer to Mohammed Ali,' Kate muttered under her breath.

'What?' He looked at her groggily.

'Never mind—just stay down or I promise I'll finish you off myself.'

It was questionable if her threat did the trick but he gave up trying to rise. Much to Kate's relief, Leyton called off his heavies and with a last stare at her, walked away towards the bar just as the club's bouncer and manager appeared.

'What's going on?' came from Brain Court.

'A misunderstanding,' Kate lamely offered.

Court pointed down at Van who now seemed distinctly unaware of what was going on round him. 'Do you know this bum?'

'Sort of,' she admitted.

'Well, darling, he comes in here again and you both go—follow?' Kate nodded compliantly before Court turned to speak to the club's doorman. 'Bounce him, Harry, and hard!'

'No, you can't!' she protested in outrage. 'He's hurt, for pity's sake—you don't need to hurt him more. He's not going to cause any more trouble.'

At least Harry hesitated, noting the way Van was holding his ribs and the sickly pallor to his complexion; Court wasn't moved at all.

'Bounce him, Harry,' he repeated, 'and make sure he doesn't want to come back in a hurry.'

'You touch him and I'll . . . I'll create such a scene you'll lose every single customer in the place,' Kate retorted, without the slightest idea of how to carry out the threat.

But it made Court stop and think before angrily giving way, 'All right. Harry, just get him on his feet and out of here. You, go back to your table!'

Kate's eyes switched from Court back to Van and she found herself saying, 'No, I'm sorry but I'll have to go with him. Can't you see he needs help?'

The appeal was wasted on Court. 'If you want to play Florence Nightingale, darling, that's your choice— but not on my time. You walk out now, don't bother to come back.'

Kate gazed up at the Genevieve's manager, wondering how she'd stood his bullying manner for so long.

'Okay, you've persuaded me,' she said, and waiting for his normally smug expression to reappear, added, 'And may I say that working for you has been the *nadir* of my whole existence.'

'The what?' Court was completely thrown, not yet realising *he* was being dismissed.

'Look it up,' Kate muttered and then proceeded to ignore him. 'Harry, will you give me a hand?' she asked and her soft pleading tone had the doorman bending to take Van's other arm.

They heaved him to his feet and he mumbled something about being able to walk but the moment Harry made to withdraw his support, the American swayed precariously. Not needing any more directions, Harry slung Van's arm round his shoulder and Kate went ahead to open the doors to the street.

There was a taxi already standing outside. Incredible good luck, Kate thought, until the driver, about to refuse the fare, recognised their burden.

'Is he okay?' the cabbie enquired anxiously, helping Kate to install him in the back.

'Never better.' Van rallied to reply for himself and less distinctly announced, 'Mission accomplished as you can see.'

With a sideways glance at Kate, the cabbie grinned before he shut the door and climbed into the front. Lips tightening, she wondered at the exchange but forgot it as Van slumped his head back on the seat.

Alarmed, she sought the friendly cabbie's opinion. 'He's passed out. Do you think we should take him to a hospital?'

Turning in his seat, the cabbie studied Van and shook his head. 'He'd have to wait hours in casualty on a Sunday night. He'd probably be better off at home and you can call out a doctor if he's still bad.'

Kate decided to take what sounded like good advice and the cabbie sped them through the late-night traffic to Van's flat. By the time they arrived, he had revived sufficiently to walk with her help but he was obviously in some pain.

'What's your doctor's number?' she demanded when she'd deposited him on the edge of his bed.

'Doctor?' He frowned up at her. 'Hell, I don't need a doctor.'

Kate decided she wasn't going to argue the point. 'Don't you think we've had enough of the John Wayne heroics for one night?' Her voice was laden with scorn and left him struggling for a reply as she repeated, 'Now—your doctor's number?'

He looked completely taken aback for a moment and then remarkably chastened. 'Okay. It's in the book by the phone. Under "d" for——'

'I think I can work it out,' she cut in briskly. 'You'd better get undressed while I telephone him.'

'What if I need some help?' he asked, daring to try a smile on her as wicked as the look in his eyes.

It was too much for Kate, slamming the door behind her as she marched out of the bedroom to the telephone in the hall. He used a private medical service and the doctor on call promised to be there within half an hour. She spent fifteen minutes of it making tea in the kitchen before returning to the bedroom. She was brought to a halt in the doorway.

He had managed to take his clothes off and prop himself up in bed but he hadn't concerned himself with anything as conventional as pyjamas. A sheet barely covered him to the waist.

'You can come in,' he said on noticing her, 'I'm decent.'

It didn't sound mocking although it could have been, Kate realised, made aware she was staring at him as though he were stark naked. Staring, not exactly shocked, at the muscular expanse of his chest, still tanned from his months abroad, and the mat of dark blond hair arrowing down to a flat abdomen.

'And safe,' he added, definitely mocking as, eyes averted, she approached the bed.

'Here.' Less than graciously she banged the cup she was carrying on his bedside table.

'What is it?' He peered into the cup.

'Tea with arsenic,' she muttered back.

'I'd sooner have a real drink.' He offered her a persuasive smile.

'Well, you know where the bloody drinks-cabinet is!' she snapped angrily and, visibly fuming, began to tidy up the room.

Surprisingly apologetic she heard, 'The tea's lovely, Kate. Thanks.'

But the words didn't soften her mood: his behaviour at the club had been inexcusable. She was furious with him, and she was going to stay that way.

'Please, Kate,' he murmured when she turned from the wardrobe, 'we have to talk.'

'Why?' She gave him a hard look. 'You did what you set out to do. There's nothing more to say. It isn't my fault you ended up getting hurt.'

'I know—I blew it,' he admitted with a groan. 'It was just that guy—the way he was watching you.'

'What guy?' Kate asked irritably.

'The one at the table,' he growled back, almost as though he was accusing her of something. 'I was sitting at the bar for a while and he never moved his eyes off you the whole time I was there.'

'So what!' she snapped back. 'How I choose to spend my time outside working hours, is my business. You have no right to interfere with my private life.'

'Yeah, I know that and I didn't intend to. In fact I told Johnny so. But dammit, Kate, you can't have wanted to work in that dump?'

'Johnny—*you told Johnny*?' she echoed.

Van raised his hands. 'Hey, hold on now, Kate. I told Johnny I couldn't interfere but it was *Johnny* who told *me* about the Genevieve.'

'How could he?' she challenged. 'He didn't know.'

'No, not until last Sunday. He followed you and your friend Sally to the place.'

'Followed us—why should he do that?'

'He says he didn't believe you were going out with anyone besides me,' Van explained in a slightly wry tone. 'Anyway, when he saw you leave the house with Sally, he decided to play detective.'

Kate was still confused. 'But when did he tell you all this?'

'A few hours ago. He telephoned Friday evening but I was visiting my sister Ellen. When I returned this afternoon I found a rather garbled message from him on my answering machine and decided to drive up to his school to talk to him in person.'

'Is he very upset?' she asked, worry replacing the initial shock.

'Well, he'd obviously been brooding about it all week but I managed to calm him down on the idea of your working in a nightclub. He was more hurt that you'd kept it a secret from him . . . He hasn't figured out why you're moonlighting, though,' Van finished, his eyes holding hers.

'And you have?' she said cagily.

'At a guess, yes, I'd say you were doing it to help raise his school fees although he seems to think they're paid out of some trust fund,' Van replied and, at her frown, added, 'I'm right, aren't I?'

Kate nodded, seeing little point in denying it. 'But if you say anything to Johnny, I'll never forgive you, Van. Never!' she repeated fiercely.

'Kate,' he sighed heavily, 'don't you know yet I only want to help you?'

'Do you? Then keep out of things, Van. Johnny shouldn't have involved you,' Kate stated, more weary than angry now, and was relieved to hear the doorbell ring.

She showed the doctor into the bedroom and left him to examine Van alone. Going to the lounge, she helped herself to a stiff drink. The examination seemed to take an age. Finally she went to wait in the hallway.

'How is he?' she enquired the moment the doctor came out.

'Oh, he'll live,' he reassured with a touch of wryness. 'His ribs are bruised and I've taped them up. I don't think any are cracked but I'll arrange an X-ray tomorrow afternoon to check. Other than that, make sure he takes the pain-killers I've left.'

'Yes, and thanks for coming out, doctor,' Kate said, showing him to the door.

'No trouble. Just try and convince Mr Fitzgerald his fighting days are over—if you can,' he added with a smile.

'I—yes,' Kate agreed, deciding that an explanation of her relationship with Mr Fitzgerald wouldn't help matters.

When she wandered back into the bedroom, a swathe of bandage was wrapped round his lower chest but he no longer seemed in actual pain.

Nevertheless she asked, 'Have you taken the pills the doctor gave you?'

'Not yet. Listen, Kate——' he began, only to be

interrupted by her muttering she would fetch some water from the adjoining bathroom.

Van, however, was determined to be heard out and when she came back to the bedside, he made a grab for her arm. 'Please, Kate, stand still for a moment.'

'I don't seem to have much choice,' Kate said after attempting unsuccessfully to escape his grip.

'Dammit, Kate, I'm trying to apologise!' he rapped out in a distinctly unapologetic tone.

'Really?' She arched a brow.

'Yes,' he controlled his rising frustration, 'I accept you have every right to be mad. I behaved like a real fool. But I want to make it up to you.'

'What do you mean?' she said suspiciously.

'Johnny's school fees, if you need money, Kate——'

'I can manage,' she cut in sharply.

'Without that other job?' His expression was concerned.

And she admitted in a softer tone, 'Yes, I was only working there till Christmas for some spending money.'

'Then let me at least give you that, Kate.' He gently squeezed her arm. 'I'd like to help you—you and Johnny. He's told me you've had a hard time since your parents died. And I wouldn't even miss the money.'

He so obviously did want to help her, Kate found herself wavering for a moment. Then she wondered how generous he would be if he knew the truth about her— the whole truth. Would he want to help Katerina St Gregory as well as plain Kate Gregory? She doubted it.

'No, thanks, I can manage,' she repeated with a weary shake of her head.

Van registered her tiredness. 'Okay, we'll talk about it tomorrow when we get up in the morning.'

'What?' Her eyes abruptly lost their drowsiness.

The reason for her shock must have been obvious as he chuckled back, 'If you're thinking what I think you're thinking, sweet Kate, I'm hardly in a fit state to justify such alarm.'

'I wasn't!' she snapped, resenting the amusement in his eyes. Was everything a joke to him?

'Good—because I don't want to have to spend all

night persuading you it's quite safe to use one of my spare bedrooms,' he went on, still with an undercurrent of laughter.

'I'd sooner go home,' she muttered, jerking her hand out of his hold.

'Like that?' His eyes ran over her cocktail dress.

One of the showy dresses she'd bought for the Genevieve, she was suddenly reminded of how lowcut it was—and that she'd walked out of the club without even collecting her coat or bag.

'Can you lend me a coat and the money for a taxi?' she asked, feeling it no more than her right.'

'Certainly not,' he replied flatly. 'Call me old-fashioned if you want, but I don't like a woman having to make her own way home at this late hour.'

Old-fashioned was hardly the phrase that passed through Kate's mind.

'And besides,' he continued, forestalling the argument he could see brewing in her eyes, 'I might need your assistance to re-strap my bandages in the morning.'

Kate could see herself being out-manoeuvred once more. 'Where are your housekeys?' she demanded shortly.

'My housekeys?' he echoed. 'They're over on the dresser . . . why?'

Kate didn't reply till she had found them and was back, safe at the bedroom door.

'Just some insurance in case your bandages get lonely during the night,' she threw over her shoulder before shutting the door behind her.

And the click of the key in the lock gave rise to her first smile of the whole night.

CHAPTER ELEVEN

KATE woke quite early in the unfamiliar bed, weak December sunlight filtering through the half-closed curtains. Lying still for a while, she listened to the birds outside, surprised to find things really could look different in the morning.

When she thought of the Genevieve, she discovered it was with relief—relief that she didn't have to go back again. And Johnny? Well, perhaps if she telephoned this evening to say she was no longer working there, it would set his mind at rest.

As for Christmas, she'd simply have to settle on buying him a more modest present. She should be grateful she had the money for his fees. A few months ago that alone hadn't seemed possible. So things weren't nearly half as tragic as they'd appeared last night.

Her self-reassurance, however, came to an end when she caught a stirring noise from next door. For a moment she was nervous he'd wander through before she had time to dress. Then recalling his locked door, she almost leapt out of bed, her boldness of last night also gone with the sanity morning brought. A way of getting the better of him and his mocking humour, now it seemed an act of sheer folly.

She grabbed an old towelling robe hanging in the wardrobe and crept out into the corridor. As stealthily as possible she fitted the key in the lock. It was a big, brass key—the master for all the rooms in the flat—and it seemed to make a very loud noise as she turned it. If he was awake he would surely have noticed.

She pressed her ear to the door and heard some sound through its panelling. Totally unexpected, she took several seconds to identify what it was.

He couldn't be groaning! she told herself, even as she tentatively pushed open the door to discover he was. Alarmed, she padded barefoot to the wide double bed. He was lying on his back, eyes closed and his face ominously pale in the shadows of the darkened room.

'Van,' she called softly from the foot of the bed.

Her quiet murmur drew another groan but his eyes remained shut. It scared her. Not once had he groaned aloud last night.

'Van!' she repeated, still low but urgent now as she knelt on the bed with the idea she should waken him.

But when she gently touched his shoulder, it evoked more of a reaction than she'd been prepared for. One second she was leaning over him, eyes wide with anxiety, the next staring *up* at him, eyes wider with astonishment.

'Morning, Kate.' His lips slanted in a devilish smile before dropping a swift hard kiss on her startled mouth.

'Why you——' Realising she'd been had, it was temper that made Kate try to push him away and this time there was nothing phoney about his immediate groan.

'Hell, Kate,' he gasped on a sharp breath as he rolled on his side, 'I was only fooling around.'

It was on the tip of her tongue to snap, 'Serves you right!' but when she turned to look at him clutching his ribs, somehow the words changed to an anxious, 'Are you okay, Van? I didn't mean to . . . I forgot . . .'

'Yeah.' He made a half-pained, half-wry grimace. 'I should have known you'd do that.'

On the defensive, Kate was stung to retort, 'What did you expect me to do?'

'Oh, I live in hope,' he drawled back, smile mocking as he began to recover and reminding Kate of her present position. She had barely formed the intention of scrambling off the bed when a hand reached out to delay her. 'Stay a moment longer, Kate. I'm harmless.' It was an appeal not a demand, and as he implied, in his condition he could hardly force her.

So why *did* she let him gently pull her round to face him? Why did she lie by his side so still she might have been a statue—or return his stare and find herself excited rather than scared by his closeness?

'Lovely Kate, you don't know how long I've imagined this—wakening in the morning to have you lying beside me, your black hair spread on my pillow . . .'

'Van——' she protested huskily but he hushed her, pressing his fingers to her lips.

'Just sweet dreams, Kate, nothing to fear.' He stroked her cheek with the back of his hand.

'Van, stop it!' This time she managed to put some firmness in the command—it made little impression.

'Why? I was just getting to the interesting part,' he complained and laughed softly at her prim expression. 'Don't you want to know what happens next?'

'I can imagine!' she claimed rashly.

'You can?' He raised his eyebrows with light mockery. 'Now that does surprise me. After all, imagination is usually based on first-hand experience and something tells me—probably the delightful blush on your cheeks—that this is a new one for you.'

'What is?' Kate was foolish enough to ask.

He took time in replying, his eyes wandering down her length before he drawled back, 'Being in bed with a man.'

A deeper blush hit Kate's face as she retorted furiously, 'I'm not *in* bed with you! I'm——'

Exasperated, Kate broke off. Why was she even listening to his nonsense? She made to rise again but he was quicker, a hand clamping down on her arm to keep her there.

'Hey, don't get mad,' he rebuked, his own tone irritatingly mild. 'I was just kidding, Kate.'

'Everything's one big joke to you, isn't it?' she scowled crossly.

'No, not everything.' He took her unawares, hands pressing her down against the pillows as he shifted to lean over her again. 'And if that's an invitation to get serious——'

'It wasn't!' Kate flared back, 'And you'd better get off me this minute or I'll . . . I'll . . .'

'You'll . . .?' he prompted, eyes still full of laughter.

'I'll give you something to really groan about,' she warned through clenced teeth.

He intercepted her glance at his bandaged ribs but after the briefest hesitation, shook his head. 'You wouldn't.'

'Try me!' she countered fiercely.

'Now that is definitely an invitation,' he chuckled as he began to lower his head.

'I will—I mean it, Van!' she insisted, her hands already curled into fists.

'Sure you do,' he agreed but so soft she barely

caught it before his head descended that last inch towards hers.

Kate had no time to think, no time to wonder at her own reactions: only feelings, feelings that swept over her like waves as his mouth claimed hers in a deeply passionate kiss; waves rising higher and higher as he began to push aside her robe; higher and higher as his hands spread against her bare skin; so high she felt she might drown if she didn't cling to him.

Yet it wasn't Van who saved her but a voice penetrating their total absorption in each other, a voice calling from the corridor, 'Mr Van, are you——'

Then dying away as Mrs O'Reilly stopped inside the open doorway, rooted with shock.

Unfortunately Van lifted his head away to half turn and together they saw the older woman's face assume a horrified mask on recognising the girl with him. And without another word, she wheeled round out of the room.

'Damn!' Van groaned as the kitchen door slammed shut at the far end of the hall.

Mortified with embarrassment, Kate choked out, 'She must have thought . . . Oh, God, what can we do?'

'Well, I don't expect she could be persuaded into believing I was giving you dictation,' Van replied on an infuriatingly wry note.

'It's not funny!' she cried back.

'No, I guess it's not,' he agreed suddenly. 'She's a good worker, Mrs O. I'd hate her to walk out over this.'

'Is that *all* that concerns you?' she gasped, watching him relax back against the pillows.

He returned her glare with a thoughtful look. 'You're worried about your reputation, right?' he said as though playing a guessing game.

Incensed, Kate scrambled off the bed. 'I'm hardly likely to be worried about yours, am I?'

'No, I reckon not,' he replied with some effort at a straight face. 'All right, I'll speak to her.'

'When?' Kate demanded.

'Is *now* soon enough?' he mocked her persistence by feigning a move to climb out of bed and at her shocked glance, added, 'Or can it wait long enough for you to get me my robe from behind the bathroom door?'

The request was quickly met. 'What are you going to say to her?' Kate asked when she'd handed him the dark towelling robe and turned her back.

'I'll explain last night's events—only I wouldn't count on her crediting them. I'm finding it difficult myself,' he confided with a short laugh.

'Van, please take this seriously,' she appealed. 'It's not simply a matter of my reputation. Mrs O looked very upset.'

'Yes, I know.' Van pulled her round to face him, no trace of humour in his voice now as he went on, 'Look, Kate, the last thing I want is anyone, including you, thinking what's going on between us is just another casual affair. Okay?'

He tilted her chin so she was forced to meet his eyes, steady and suddenly very grave, and she found herself echoing, 'Okay.'

'I'll sort it out,' he promised. 'You wait here.'

She waited eight minutes, knowing precisely how long as she checked her watch every thirty seconds—trying to keep her mind off what had happened since she'd woken that morning.

It all made no sense. After last night, her feelings should have hardened against him. So why with every furious pose she took, did it seem more and more just that—a pose?

'Did she believe you?' she asked when he returned, firmly closing the door behind him.

He leaned against its frame, seeming in no hurry to reply.

'She didn't,' Kate concluded with a sigh.

'Not entirely,' he admitted carefully.

She frowned, sensing evasion. 'How much then?'

'Well, to be honest . . .' he hesitated before giving her a rueful glance, '. . . I didn't exactly tell her the full story. In fact I had a problem getting a word in edgeways. She's obviously very fond of you, is Mrs O.'

'What's that supposed to mean?' Kate's frown deepened.

'I'm just explaining how difficult it was. The moment I walked into the kitchen she was delivering a lecture on my moral degeneration,' he relayed, lips twisting at the memory. 'All about being willing to turn a blind eye to my occasional ... profligacy, I think she called it, but not when it came to my seducing sweet young things like you. By the time she was finished, she had me feeling guilty as hell and almost convinced I had.'

'But you told her you hadn't,' Kate insisted.

Again he hesitated. 'Not in so many words,' he eventually admitted. 'She wasn't about to listen, Kate. I was lucky to talk her out of leaving.'

'Then what *did* you say?' she demanded irritably, patience worn thin.

'That things weren't as bad as they might seem. And that you and I were serious and ... well, that we were considering getting hitched,' he finished with a wry grimace.

'You said *what*!' exclaimed Kate, astounded.

'I said that we were——' he actually began to repeat it.

'I heard what you said!' Kate's voice shook with suppressed rage. 'I just didn't believe it.'

He slanted her a searching look. 'You don't like the idea?'

'Like it?' She gaped at him incredulously. 'That has to be *the* most idiotic excuse you could have found for something we weren't even bloody well doing. And you need to ask if I like it?'

His mouth went into a tight line at her sarcasm. 'That wasn't quite what I meant.'

Puzzled, Kate began to mutter, 'I don't see——'

'No, so skip it!' he interrupted with a sudden harshness that made her blink. 'If you think you can do better with Mrs O, don't let me stop you.'

'I won't,' she flashed back.

Abruptly he stepped away from the door and held it open for her, a mocking challenge. Defiance rather than confidence impelled her to meet it. After all, how was she going to explain things now he'd made them worse?

'By the way,' he delayed her on the threshold and

destroyed her confidence totally with, 'I suggest you try and remember when you're protesting your innocence, sweet Kate, that if we weren't *bloody well* doing anything, we were giving a damn good impression of being about to.'

'I—I wasn't,' Kate stammered in denial, shamed colour flooding her cheeks.

'Giving a good impression or about to?' he shot back.

'I—I——' This time she faltered altogether.

'Never mind. You can tell me which when you report back,' he drawled at her evident speechlessness and nearly pushed her out of the room.

Her last glimpse of his face, however, told Kate that his insufferable humour had been restored at her expense. Some fifteen minutes later she could still recall it—that wicked, slanting grin of his—but now she appreciated its significance. She was almost certain he'd known how her talk with Mrs O'Reilly would go. In fact, certain enough not to bother reporting back. It was Van who came to find her, sitting in the spare bedroom, feeling silly in her cheap cocktail dress.

'Ah, here we are!' he announced as though she'd been hiding away.

Kate noted he, too, was dressed and shaved, but apart from that quick glance as he entered, she barely acknowledged him.

'Well?' he prompted.

'Well what?' she muttered.

'Everything straightened out, I take it,' he went on, his tone insidiously pleasant.

'Not entirely,' she admitted.

'How much then?' he returned.

Hearing echoes of their earlier conversation, Kate's head jerked up, but if he was mocking her, he concealed it well. His face was a picture of innocence. Nevertheless, she lapsed back into silent contemplation of the wallpaper pattern, and tensed as he came to sit beside her on the bed.

'Come on, Kate, we have to at least get our stories straight. Did she give you a rough time? Is that why you're upset?'

'No, not really. She said . . .'

'She said what, Kate?' A hand lightly gripped her chin to force her to look at him. 'Listen, if she's going to be hard on you, I'll tell her she can walk out now.'

Realising he meant it, Kate hastily denied, 'No, she was actually very nice about it. In fact before I could get a word out, she—you won't laugh, will you?'

'Cross my heart,' he said with an unusual solemnity.

'She said she wasn't so old she couldn't remember what it was like to be young and . . . and in love. And now she knew you weren't simply taking advantage, she was very pleased for us both because . . . because she's always thought we'd be right for each other.'

'How romantic! What did you say?'

'What could I say?' Kate appealed on a defensive note. 'By the time she'd finished congratulating us, you'd have thought we'd taken out an announcement in *The Times* not . . .'

'You didn't say anything—did you?' Van surmised with a suspiciously satisfied smile.

'No, not unless you include thanking her for her good wishes,' Kate admitted dolefully.

'You thanked her?' he echoed, the smile spreading.

'Yes—and *you* promised not to laugh,' she reminded him threateningly.

'I know but——'

'*Van!*' Her glare was not sufficient to curb the amusement, lurking so clearly in his lazy blue eyes.

Hysteria, Kate thought, on realising she was the first to actually laugh aloud. But soon they were both laughing together—laughing like children caught out in a prank. No longer antagonists, suddenly conspirators.

An impression confirmed by Van chuckling, 'What a cowardly pair we are.'

'Hopeless,' Kate agreed on an amused groan. 'What are we going to do, Van? We can't possibly keep a pretence like this up for long?'

'No?' he queried but at her quick scowl, sighed, 'No, I guess not. All right, the first chance one of us gets, we tell her the whole story.'

He made it sound simple. She almost convinced

herself it was when he insisted on driving her home to change her clothes for work. But by the time they returned to the flat, it was no longer quite so simple.

The moment they closed the front door, Mrs O'Reilly appeared from the kitchen to declare in a rush, 'Oh, Mr Van, I'm glad you're back—sure I've done a terrible thing,' and then proceeded to confess her 'crime'.

Apparently Van's sister had called while they were away. Aware he had visited her at the weekend, Mrs O had assumed Lady Ellen knew all about their engagement and had told her Van was out with his fiancée. Naturally Van's sister was astounded by the news.

'Don't worry about it,' Van shrugged both to Mrs O'Reilly and to Kate when she followed him into the study.

'But surely your sister's going to be upset,' she argued as, evidently unconcerned, he settled himself behind his desk.

'Not El,' he chuckled back. 'She's dedicated a considerable amount of time and energy to getting me married off. Believe me, she'll be delighted.'

'You're missing the point—you're not getting married,' she retorted heavily.

'Yes, I guess that does make it a little awkward,' he conceded with the same exasperating mildness. 'I don't suppose you'd consider——'

'No!' snapped Kate, not sure what he was about to propose but knowing she wouldn't like it.

'Okay, okay. Cool down,' he grinned, holding his hands up in surrender. 'I'll sort it out with her.'

'When?' Kate had been singularly unimpressed with his efforts in Mrs O's direction.

'When she phones again.' He glanced at the gold watch on his wrist. 'In the next hour or so, I reckon.'

He reckoned fairly accurately, but Kate was also justified in her doubts over his talent for sorting things out. In fairness, he was hardly given the chance. Even from across the room, she could hear the stream of chatter on the other end of the line, defying much interruption. She could not distinguish his sister's actual words but her face became stonier and stonier at Van's replies.

'Yes, she's English ... my secretary, that's right ... I know but I didn't want you scaring her off with the third degree, sis ... she's about twenty-two ... no, not a blonde—jet black hair, dark brown eyes and absolutely gorgeous ...' The brief description was offered to his sister but it was a glaring Kate who was subjected to his appraisal while he continued to answer a barrage of questions, '... maybe it is time ... Christmas? ... no, she hasn't any folks ... I'll ask ... she's here now, yes ...'

Then putting his hand over the mouthpiece, he held out the receiver to Kate. 'My sister wants to speak to you.'

'But what do you expect me to say?' she protested, well aware he had yet to deny their engagement.

'Please, Kate, I can't explain the mix-up over the phone. Just say hello, huh?'

About to refuse outright, Kate suddenly remembered how decently he had behaved with Johnny in similar circumstances. Reluctantly she crossed to murmur a tentative greeting into the telephone and quickly discovered thinking about what else to say, was the least of her worries.

It wasn't so much that his sister dominated a conversation as flitted between sentences with a charming illogicality. Following her alone took all Kate's concentration. That she was highly delighted by the engagement was resoundingly clear. So clear, it was exceedingly difficult to deny it and impossible to get out of an invitation to spend Christmas and New Year at Ashbourne Manor, the home of Ellen's aristocratic husband. Mention of Johnny, as an excuse, only had him included in the invitation, with the assurance that Ellen's two teenage sons would be company for him. And before she could find another excuse, Van reclaimed the telephone, promising he would persuade her to go. It seemed a rash promise to make but not until he'd rung off did Kate realise he intended to keep it.

'Is Johnny home by the twenty-first?' he asked and

when Kate nodded, informed her, 'I usually go down a few days before Christmas.'

Then Kate began to shake her head. 'Oh no, if you mean what I think you mean, forget it.'

'Come on, Kate,' he cajoled, catching her arm to prevent her retreating back to her desk, 'you heard how pleased she is. I couldn't blurt out the truth, now could I? If you came out with me for the holiday, we could both break it to her gently ... And Johnny too, he would have a great time with the boys.'

'No, Van, and leave Johnny out of this. I'm not going.'

'But why not?' he asked as though her refusal was unreasonable.

'Because I——' Kate started to justify it, paused for thought and at his flicker of a smile, stated categorically, 'I don't intend to discuss it. I'm not going and that's final.'

'Okay.' He shrugged after a brief hesitation.

She waited for more. None was forthcoming. Evidently he wasn't going to pursue it further. Kate was disconcerted by his easy capitulation—even a little piqued. But she was not suspicious.

She should have known better.

CHAPTER TWELVE

ASHBOURNE MANOR, the ancestral home of the sixth Earl of Sanderford, was not in itself a beautiful building. Its ancient grey stone and towering symmetry made it seem a bleak rather than gracious house. The grounds, however, were another matter.

They approached by a side road twisting through woodland to find the house set above a spectacular view of ornamental gardens. Laid out in geometric patterns with shrubs, flowers and small evergreens, even in winter their landscaping compensated for the Manor's grim appearance.

'Wow!' Johnny exclaimed as they drew to a halt on the forecourt, and pointing to some massive hedging on the right of the gardens, enquired in awed tones, 'Is that a maze, Van?'

'Sure is,' the American confirmed.

'Wow!' Johnny said a second time and then a third, when he was told there were tennis courts behind it.

Kate said nothing. She sat shrinking in the front seat, wondering why she was there at all. When Johnny clambered out of the back seat, she made no move to follow.

Van used the opportunity to murmur, 'You're not still sulking with me, are you?'

'No, I am *not sulking*,' she ground out, 'I'm seething. Not that I'd expect you to appreciate the difference.'

He drew in a deep breath and let it out on a sigh. 'As a matter of fact I do, and for what it's worth, I admit it was a dirty trick to pull.'

A dirty trick! That was the understatement of the year. For almost a fortnight after his sister's call, he had suddenly reverted to being friendly and no more. Then three days ago, he had offered to drive her to Suffolk to collect Johnny from school.

A kind, considerate gesture she'd thought—until he not only told her brother about the invitation to spend Christmas with his family but made it sound as though Kate was hesitating solely on his account. And before she could deny it, Johnny was giving his enthusiastic support for the idea.

Later she'd given her brother a censored version of the events leading up to this invitation, ensuring he understood that there was no real engagement, but it had not discouraged his enthusiasm for the visit. He was already grateful to Van for *persuading* her to stop working in the nightclub, and now he seemed to think she should help the American out in turn. So here they were.

Several figures appeared in the arched doorway to divert her thoughts and her sullen look became a positive scowl.

Nervously Van added, 'You're not going to act funny in front of my family, are you, Kate?'

'You want to see how funny I can be?' she threw back.

'*Kate!*' It was half-plea, half-threat, said as she began to climb out of the car.

Kate didn't reply. Let him stew, she thought, knowing perfectly well she wouldn't behave badly. Johnny's presence alone guaranteed that. And anyway, her argument wasn't with his sister.

She liked her from the first. A tall blonde, looking younger than her forty years, Lady Ellen Dryden had no airs and graces about her. While Van's attention was claimed by an over-enthusiastic Irish wolfhound and two equally enthusiastic teenagers, she introduced herself with a warm smile, apologised for her husband not being there to welcome them, and identified the teenagers as her sons, Rick and Stephen.

And if the house was austere from the outside, the inside was welcoming. Ellen led them into a pleasant room with old-fashioned furnishings, a blazing log fire and a large Christmas tree, standing in front of one set of bay windows. It had a family atmosphere, as did the afternoon tea that greeted their arrival.

The two boys, Rick and Stephen, wolfed down sandwiches and cake as though they hadn't eaten for days, and after a brief sizing up of Johnny, began to ask him questions. Johnny seemed to find nothing odd about being quizzed on his abilities at table tennis, Monopoly and computer Star Wars; and before Kate had time to worry whether he would fit in, he had disappeared with the others to the games room in the attic.

'Blessed peace,' Ellen sighed when they were gone.

Laughing, Van pointed out, 'They've only been home three days.'

'Yes, I know, and I've been dying to see them. But can they be exhausting!' Ellen rolled her eyes expressively. 'Especially Stephen—he just needs to look at something and it breaks. Yesterday it was that grotesque vase that used to stand on the upper gallery.

God only knows what Tommy's going to say when he gets back to find another family heirloom gone.'

Tommy was the sixth earl who, Kate had already gathered, was 'something in the Foreign Office' and had been called to Washington for a few days.

'Maybe he won't notice,' Van suggested.

'That's what I'm hoping,' Ellen confided with a wicked smile very like her brother's. 'Anyway, forget about my problems. I'd sooner hear all about your plans.'

'Plans?' Kate echoed as the remark was directed at her.

'For the wedding,' Ellen supplied and then misinterpreting the agitated glance that flashed from Kate to Van, 'You're not going to cheat Kate out of a white wedding, are you, Van?'

'Not exactly,' he hedged. 'It's just that we have one or two problems of our own, El.'

Kate frowned, wondering what was coming next, but Ellen forestalled it with, 'Look, if it's a simple matter of arrangements, I'd love to have you married from here. In fact I was going to suggest it. I've already asked Tommy and he's more than agreeable.'

'That's sweet of you, El,' Van smiled back, 'and we sure appreciate it, but things aren't quite settled between Kate and me.'

Kate could only stare in dumb astonishment when he proceeded to confess the truth to his sister, and with a blend of humour and apology that had Ellen sympathetic, if disappointed.

'I don't suppose I gave you a chance to tell me all this when I called,' she admitted graciously.

'Not much,' Van teased.

Kate, however, felt bound to add, 'I'm awfully sorry. I should have said something when you invited me to stay. I wasn't going to come but——'

'I persuaded her,' Van inserted quickly, 'and before she decides to hightail it back to London, please tell her she's welcome sis.'

'Of course you are,' asserted Ellen and on an amused note, declared, 'You may not be crazy enough to take my brother on permanently but working for him alone, probably entitles you to the break.'

'Thanks, El,' Van laughed drily. 'We may not be engaged but don't put her off completely, huh?'

'Oh,' Ellen murmured, eyes speculative as they moved between the two. 'Then you are . . . friends.'

'Some of the time,' Van replied cryptically and avoided any further questions by rising to his feet. 'I'll show Kate up to her room if that's okay.'

'Sure. I'll get someone to take your bags up.' Ellen escorted them to the foot of the stairs, and murmuring to Van which rooms were prepared, left him to act as host.

Kate's was situated in the far corner of the upper gallery, a large high-ceilinged room with heavy oak furniture dominated by a four poster. A fire burned brightly in an old-fashioned hearth to take the chill from the air but she gravitated towards a window looking out over the parkland at the rear of the house.

Van came to stand at her shoulder. 'Still mad at me?'

Kate shook her head but her forehead remained creased in a frown. 'I just don't understand what you're playing at, Van.'

'You wanted me to tell her, didn't you?'

'Yes, of course I did,' she agreed, turning to face him. 'But you must have known it wouldn't be that difficult to explain things to your sister. So why am I here?'

'That's obvious surely,' he muttered, an exasperated edge to his voice.

Resenting it, she snapped back, 'To you, maybe.'

'Dammit, Kate, why do you think?'

'I don't know!'

'All right, I'll spell it out for you. You're here because I want to spend Christmas with you. And I want to do that because—well I want to, that's all!'

He finished on such an abrupt impatient note Kate couldn't believe he really meant what he said. But she decided, for once, not to argue back.

'Now why don't you change into something warmer and we'll take a stroll in the gardens?' he went on more evenly, and wandered out of the room, leaving Kate as confused as ever.

He reappeared some fifteen minutes later but this time from a side door rather than the one leading to the corridor.

'We have adjoining rooms,' he answered her slightly startled look, and then claimed with an undercurrent of laughter, 'Not my doing, I swear it. Ellen made certain assumptions. But don't worry about it.'

'Oh, I won't,' she retorted, head at a haughty angle, 'as long as Ellen is the only one making assumptions.'

'Ouch!' he muttered, although plainly more amused than anything by her cutting remark. 'Now you've put me in my place, sweet Kate, do you suppose you could relax and enjoy yourself?'

Kate doubted it very much, feeling her own place in this family gathering ambiguous, to say the least.

Yet she was wrong: it was impossible not to relax in the easy-going Dryden household and join in the lively conversation sustained throughout dinner. From their frequent laughter, Johnny was evidently getting on well with the other two boys and Kate herself very quickly developed a soft spot for the accident-prone Stephen, with his shock of blond hair and mischievous blue eyes.

'He's a pest,' Ellen laughed when the boys raced off to fetch their Monopoly set.

'Not at all,' Kate denied, still smiling at some of his boyish confidences. 'I think he's lovely.'

'Despite the resemblance?' Van inserted, eyes glinting with amusement.

But his mockery rebounded on him when, ignoring his groans, Ellen dug out some snaps that confirmed Van had been very like Stephen at the same age.

'How cute!' Kate commented, much to Van's disgust, and though she'd said it to provoke that reaction, she thought it, too.

Encouraged, Ellen also showed her pictures of their mother who died when they were young and from whom they had inherited their blonde good looks. Their important father, however, did not appear in any of the old photographs. It made Kate think Ellen might share

Van's dislike of him but a later conversation suggested she had a more tolerant attitude.

The Monopoly board had been set up in a far corner of the room and the game in progress was interspersed with light squabbles usually settled by Van. Seated by the fire, the two women's eyes were drawn by a sudden burst of laughter.

'The boys always enjoy Christmas with Van around,' Ellen remarked affectionately.

'Does he come every year?' Kate smiled back.

'Well, no ...' Ellen hesitated before admitting, '... not if our father comes instead.'

Sensing her slight embarrassment, Kate murmured, 'Van did tell me he and your father hadn't seen each other for a long time.'

'Yes, too long, I'm afraid. I've tried arranging a reconciliation but Van's not interested.' Ellen gave a helpless shrug. 'Not that I blame him really. Our father isn't the most agreeable of characters and he behaved very unreasonably over Van's decision to become a correspondent instead of following him into politics.'

'What did he do?' Kate asked, her curiosity roused.

'Oh, he used his influence to get Van fired from the first newspaper that hired him, then a second and a third until Van finally wised up and started writing under a different name.' Ellen sighed over her father's actions. 'The funny thing is I think he was convinced he was acting in Van's best interests. To him, Van was giving up a possibly brilliant future.'

'How does he feel now?'

'I'm not sure. I know he wants to see Van. I believe he wrote to him after he came back from Africa earlier this year. But Van doesn't seem prepared to meet him halfway.' Ellen shook her head, then switched abruptly to another subject as the rest joined them, their game finished.

Watching Van laugh as the boys teased him for being the loser, Kate was surprised he was so unforgiving towards his father. Thirteen years was a long time to keep up a quarrel. Still, it was really none of her business, she decided, with no premonition of how soon it would be.

The next day Ellen insisted the boys spend the day helping her to deliver toys which the Women's Institute had collected for the local Children's Home. Kate was whisked off by Van to Guildford for Christmas shopping. She had already bought modest presents for his family and a gadgety digital watch for Johnny but she was dragged round the shops while Van consulted her on his. Well, *dragged* to begin with until she was infected by his good humour.

There was a single wrong note in the afternoon's outing. After selecting suitable presents for his family, he turned his attention to Johnny. It was not that unexpected he might buy her brother something but his suggestion staggered her.

'No!' she refused bluntly, the price ticket on the computer making her gasp.

His brow creased at her abruptness. 'I thought he was into this sort of thing.'

'Yes, but you can't possibly——' Kate broke off to search for a more tactful refusal, 'I mean it's too generous compared with what you bought for Rick and Stephen. They are your nephews and——'

'And likely to get more presents than's good for them from their English relations,' he firmly overrode her objections. 'Look, I like your kid brother. I want to get him something. If you're worried about the others, we'll say it came from you.'

He went ahead and bought it, handing the wrapped parcel to her. Kate wasn't given any choice but to take it.

There was a constrained silence between them on the way home until Kate finally mumbled, 'I'm sorry about the fuss I made over Johnny's present.'

Van shrugged. 'Forget it. Maybe you thought I was trying to buy myself into your good books—and maybe I was.'

'But you don't need to do that!' she exclaimed impulsively and drew his eyes from the road in a startled glance.

'Now I wonder what to make of that,' he eventually murmured.

Kate, however, didn't volunteer more. It was enough of a shock realising what she had meant, accepting that somewhere along the line, she had stopped thinking him that brash, arrogant, impossible American. She did not want to analyse her feelings further.

'Tommy's back early,' Van said as they pulled up in the Manor forecourt beside a smart Daimler.

Kate felt slightly nervous about meeting the sixth earl, even if Van had described him as being an 'amusing guy' underneath the stiff British upper lip. Imagining Ellen would be preoccupied with her husband, it was surprising to find her waiting for them in the hall. Her face was harrowed as she dismissed the young maid evidently assigned to watch for their return.

'Van, I don't know how to tell you this——' she began, her hands gesturing despair. 'It wasn't planned, I swear it. Tommy ran into him in Washington and he simply invited himself at the last minute. And Tommy tried to phone but . . .' Ellen trailed off because Van was clearly no longer listening.

Kate saw his features hardening, without realising why. It took her several more seconds and the sudden appearance of two figures in the sitting-room doorway for her to understand.

Tommy Dryden she recognised from his photo-graph—how she knew the other man was Senator Fitzgerald, was not so easy to explain.

There was certainly no family resemblance. His angular face might once have been considered hand-some, but in a very severe sort of way. And his eyes, flicking between Van and her, were a cold humourless grey.

For a moment no one spoke while Van exchanged a hostile, measuring look with his father. Then the Senator took the initiative, and came forward, hand outstretched.

'Sullivan,' he acknowledged his son.

After a noticeable hesitation, Van accepted the handshake with a bare nod of, 'Sir.'

There was no warmth in either man's voice.

'And this must be the fiancée I've heard of,' the Senator prompted.

Kate waited for a cue from Van. She wasn't over-surprised to hear him say, 'Yes, this is Kate—Kate Gregory,' and meeting those cold grey eyes again, she didn't blame Van for not rushing into a denial.

For if the Senator gave no sign of approving the supposed engagement, she couldn't imagine him being amused by the true situation either. In fact she couldn't imagine him being amused, full stop.

'Miss Gregory,' he inclined his head fractionally. 'Congratulations—I understand you were my son's secretary.'

It was said with what might pass for a smile but there was something very pointed in the way he congratulated her rather than Van.

'Yes, actually I still am,' Kate replied, forcing herself to be polite. 'How do you do, Mr Fitzgerald?'

The Senator ignored the enquiry but he did give her a speculative look which noted the bare fingers of one hand even while he briefly shook the other.

'I see you haven't managed to get my son to make things official yet,' he commented with unmistakable cynicism.

Kate would have let the remark go but Van almost growled, 'It's official enough. Kate doesn't need a ring to know how I feel.'

'Then she must be unique to her sex,' the Senator said, now more on a sneer than a smile.

'She is,' Van asserted, his voice unusually harsh, 'but I don't expect you to appreciate it. So if you'll excuse us . . .'

'Van!' It was Ellen who called him back as he strode to the stairs with Kate.

'Just going to change for dinner, El,' he explained briefly, reading the concern in her eyes. Then glancing at his English brother-in-law, greeted, 'Good to see you, Tommy.'

'And you,' Tommy smiled back. 'Hurry down—and I'll start mixing the Martinis.'

Van nodded before continuing up the stairs, a guiding hand at Kate's elbow. When they reached her room, he turned to face her and appealed in a grim voice, 'What can I say, Kate? I'm sorry—if I'd known he was coming . . .'

'You'd not be here,' she finished for him.

'Yeah, I guess that much was obvious,' he sighed heavily. 'I certainly didn't want to put you through this experience. The Senator tends to have a very unnerving affect on the uninitiated.'

'I can imagine,' she muttered under her breath, but Van caught it.

'Goddamn awful, isn't he?' he groaned, and had Kate wavering between a tactful and an honest reply.

Honesty won as she agreed drily, 'I'm afraid so.'

The right choice, for it made him smile, 'God, I'm glad you're on my side, Kate girl,' and curiously that's how Kate felt—on his side against that old man downstairs.

'Ellen doesn't seem to have told him we're not really engaged,' she pointed out softly.

'No.' His face sobered but the warmth in his eyes remained as he murmured, 'Do you mind so very much?'

Kate thought she knew what he was asking. She recalled how inadequate her own father had made her feel. And on brief acquaintance with Van's, she was certain his contempt would be as cutting for the silly way the misunderstanding had developed.

She shook her head. 'I suppose I can explain things to Johnny but what about your sister?'

'El—she won't split on us. If you haven't noticed, she still has hopes.'

'Hopes?' she echoed.

'That we'll get married. She likes you a lot, Kate—thinks we're good together,' he added with a smile she took to be teasing.

Kate gave him a cynical look in return. 'Well, Ellen might think so but your father has other ideas.'

'Like what?' Van's voice hardened.

'Like I'm a little nonentity of a secretary who's struck a goldmine—namely you,' she expanded. 'And don't tell me I'm imagining it.'

His eyes narrowed in anger at his father. 'I should have known you're too astute to miss his digs. But don't let them upset you, Kate. I'd never think it.'

'Think what precisely?' she asked.

'That you're marrying me for my money,' he supplied with a wry grimace.

'But I'm not,' she found herself having to say.

'No? Well, exactly.' And before Kate could reply, he ran on, 'We'd better get changed. Knock on my door when you're ready and we'll go down together.'

Into battle? Kate wondered grimly.

But she soon realised it was going to be a colder sort of war when she was seated across the dinner table from the Senator, wishing she could have shared the boys' more informal meal in the kitchen.

From the outset the Senator's presence had the oddest affect on Van, reducing his normally easy conversation to stilted responses. And when his father began to challenge him on his future plans, Kate could see the tension building up in him.

It was there in the mouth going into a tighter and tighter line each time the Senator addressed him. She half expected him to explode at any moment, almost wished he would instead of letting his father get to him that way. But he sat there, shrugging vague uncertain answers with no mention of his nearly completed novel, as though it could not be considered important.

Gradually the Senator turned his attention to Kate—the kind of attention she would rather have done without. For if his occasional remarks to her were never quite rude, they were often double-edged. At first she pretended to understand only their surface meaning but when she saw her politeness was taken for stupidity, pride got the better of her.

From then on, though she was never quite rude either, her replies were just as ambiguous. Her reward was the Senator's increasing disconcertment while he tried to decide if, behind her cool smile, she was being as snide as he was. Her encouragement was Van's smiling—no, smirking—at the fact that she was, and the sudden change in him as he visibly relaxed.

Still, it wasn't the most pleasant way to spend the time—trading subtle insults and hostile stares—and whenever she could, she avoided contact with the older American in the next days. Apart from in the evenings, it wasn't that difficult.

Van seemed intent on doing the same, and together they went for long walks in the grounds or joined the boys hiding in the attic or simply found a bolt-hole of their own where they could talk idly.

And if at times she wondered why he never took advantage of their solitude, at times felt so close to him she couldn't believe he didn't feel the same, she knew she should be relieved he didn't seem to want more than friendship now. For she could not allow herself to imagine that their quiet intimacy meant anything. She sensed it wouldn't last.

Every time she caught the Senator's eyes on her, they told her so. And though the man was cold and arrogant and humourless, he could not be dismissed as a fool. It was Christmas Eve before he made a direct attack.

Tommy had been called into London on some emergency and Van had gone into Guildford with Ellen for some last-minute Christmas shopping. Kate was alone in the library, perched on a windowseat reading, when she looked up to discover the Senator in the doorway, watching her.

'Good afternoon,' he muttered stiffly.

She echoed his words, and pleasantries over, she waited.

She was almost prepared for what came next. Though Ellen had confessed to relaying news of their engagement weeks ago, it was already quite clear the Senator's visit had not been prompted by any desire to welcome Kate into the family. And he proceeded to make it even clearer that he regarded her as little more than a minor inconvenience that interfered with his plans for Van's future.

Plans that had been postponed for thirteen years but were to be resurrected now Van had been forced to stop wasting his time in quixotic adventures, as the Senator termed his correspondence work. Plans that did not include one English girl who might keep his son on the wrong side of the Atlantic.

Silent while he coldly outlined them, Kate supposed his ambition for Van might be a form of love, the only expression a man like the Senator could make.

'You're right—I have no intention of leaving England,' she affirmed coolly. 'But, as for the rest, I suggest you discuss it with Van. He's perfectly capable of deciding his future for himself.'

'Is he?' The Senator blocked the doorway as she tried to sweep past him. 'Come, Miss Gregory, even I can see you have him totally infatuated. Which is why I will do everything in my power to stop him ruining his life by marrying you.'

'And how do you propose to do that, Senator?' Kate refused to be intimidated.

But her haughty question was met with a satisfied sneer of, 'Quite simply, Miss—Gregory—or do you prefer St Gregory. A more distinctive name I would have thought?'

Kate's eyes widened in stunned disbelief. 'How could you——'

'I knew everything about you, Miss St Gregory, before I arrived,' the Senator cut in, a hand reaching into his suit pocket. 'Here—it makes interesting reading.'

A letter was thrust under her nose. Automatically Kate accepted it, her fingers shaking slightly as she unfolded the paper. It didn't take long to scan the familiar contents—the details of her father's arms deals, an account of her part in the last abortive one, even mention of the debts she'd left behind on her disappearance. And if the final paragraph implied some doubt as to the extent of her complicity, it was hardly a statement of her innocence.

'I had you investigated as a matter of course,' the Senator continued while she read through the report. 'I must admit I wasn't anticipating our agents in London uncovering anything of *this* nature.'

Kate raised puzzled eyes from the letter. 'I don't understand. Why did you wait?'

'I wanted to assess the situation between you and my son for myself. I trust you won't try to deny the report?'

Kate shook her head, sensing any appeal would be wasted on this man. She didn't really care about him or what he thought of her. Only one person's opinion mattered—mattered so much tears filled her eyes in that revealing moment when she realised why.

'Are you going to show him this?' she choked out.

'If you force me to,' the Senator nodded. 'But I'd prefer you spare us both the unpleasantness and fade quietly out of his life. You see my son has some very idealistic views on people capitalising on war, and from personal experience, I can assure you he won't forgive what's in that report.'

The Senator's confident assertion confirmed what Kate had always feared. With a last shred of dignity, she refolded the letter and handed it back. He was disconcerted by the restrained gesture, by the silent tears slipping down her face. When she groped blindly for the door, he reached it first.

'Whether you believe it or not, Miss Gregory, my sole purpose in doing this is to protect Sullivan and his future,' he declared before opening the door for her. But they both froze on its threshold at the sight of Van crossing the hall.

Evidently he'd been looking for Kate, the quick smile of greeting dying on his lips when he saw her stricken face. Through her tears, she glimpsed a look of such tenderness and concern, she might have been tempted to trust his being on *her side* when she needed it. Then his eyes flicked to his father and it was gone.

'Kate!' he called after her, but it didn't halt her flight. Nor did his thunderously angry shout of, 'You bastard—what the hell have you been saying to her?'

She didn't stop until she was in her room and able to let the tears flood out. To cry into her pillow, over and over, 'I don't care!' as though the words could make it so and kill the longing for something she'd never really had and never would have now.

The love of a man so dearly worth knowing.

CHAPTER THIRTEEN

WHEN the knock on her door came later, Kate was already acting in the only possible way to hold on to her pride at least.

Ellen poked her head round the door and caught her with an armful of clothes, intended for the open suitcase on the bed.

'Kate? Why are you packing?' Ellen said in an astounded voice.

'I—I'm sorry, I have to leave.' She gave no excuses. 'Do you know where Johnny is?'

'In the attic I think—but, for God's sake, Kate, what's going on?' Ellen appealed, crossing to her side. 'You're leaving and Van and the Senator are downstairs yelling like a couple of madmen. Or Van is—for once the Senator isn't getting much of a chance to say anything.'

'He'll say enough,' Kate muttered in angry despair.

'About you?' Ellen received a brief nod. 'But you mustn't let him drive you away, Kate. Whatever he's saying, it won't affect Van's feelings for you.'

A flicker of pain darkened Kate's eyes. 'There was never really anything between us, you know,' she said, almost as if she had now to remind herself. 'It was like Van said—a misunderstanding.'

'You can't believe that. Anyone can see that he's crazy about you, Kate. And as for the Senator, well, he's just having a hard time accepting he has no influence over Van any more.'

'Hasn't he?' The image of the Senator browbeating Van at meals made Kate sceptical.

Ellen read her thoughts with a short laugh. 'Oh, don't be taken in by the way Van's been behaving. That's what's termed passive resistance. And anyway, it sounds as if his temper's finally blown.'

'Perhaps, but it may not be directed entirely at your

father.' Kate voiced her fears aloud and at Ellen's frown, explained, 'There were certain things about me that Van didn't know. I think he'll be angry I didn't tell him before the Senator.'

'I don't follow—how does my father know anything about you?' asked Ellen, more confused than ever. 'You only met a few days ago.'

'He had me investigated after you first told him of our engagement,' Kate said bitterly.

'Oh Kate!' the older woman groaned. 'What you must think of us! I should have guessed he'd do something awful like that. I don't know how to begin apologising——'

'Please, there's no need,' Kate interrupted hastily. 'I don't think you understand. The investigation he had done on me—it uncovered a lot of things . . .'

Ellen waited for her to go on, and sinking down on the edge of the bed, Kate found herself confessing what was in the report. By the end Ellen was sitting beside her.

'You should have told Van all this,' she sighed. 'Lord knows, with an unscrupulous man like the Senator for a father, he'd be the last person to condemn you for something yours did.'

'Don't you see—I helped my father,' Kate pointed out the difference.

'But without *realising* you did,' Ellen stressed, absolutely convinced of it. 'And Van's going to believe that too, Kate.'

'Will he?' Kate could recall other times when Van had thought the worst of her on less evidence.

'Well, you're about to get your chance to find out,' Ellen murmured, eyes glancing past her.

Kate swivelled round to discover Van standing in the doorway. Impossible to judge how long he'd been there or what mood he was in. His face held no expression.

Ellen didn't seem over-concerned, demanding, 'Van, where have you been? You haven't been shouting at each other all this time, have you?'

'Not quite,' he said in a dry voice. 'We reached a civilised volume in the end . . . and an understanding of sorts.'

'Meaning?' Ellen queried as he approached the foot of the bed.

'I'll tell you later. Right now, I'd like to speak to Kate,' he said, his eyes switching to her.

Ellen made no move to leave, however, until Van added, 'Alone if you don't mind, El.'

'If Kate doesn't?' she gazed enquiringly at the other girl.

Kate was tempted to ask her to stay. She still couldn't read Van's mood even though he was staring right at her. She might have felt less nervous if he'd shown himself to be blazingly angry.

'She doesn't,' Van answered for her, 'and I think the Senator may need your peacemaking talents, Sis.'

'God, that sounds ominous,' Ellen groaned as she rose to her feet. 'Just make sure Kate doesn't when you've finished, brother dear.'

The silence also seemed ominous when she'd gone. Kate dropped her eyes back to her lap. She didn't know what to say or if she should say anything.

Eventually Van picked up his sister's parting shot by musing, 'I wonder what she thinks I'm going to do to you.'

And hearing its suspiciously wry note, Kate's eyes lifted back to his in disbelief. Surely he wasn't going to laugh this off too? Or did he simply not care who or what she was?

'Did your father show you it—a report on me?'

'Yes, I had a skim through it,' he returned mildly. 'I'm afraid my reaction rather disappointed him.'

His reaction wasn't doing much for Kate either. Crazy though it probably was, she would have preferred his black temper to this indifference.

Crazier still, she found herself almost boasting, 'It's all true, you know.'

'Is it?' The quiet murmur seemed equally offhand.

'Yes, and I'm not about to apologise for any of it either,' she added, her manner stiff with pride.

'Dear Kate, an apology is the last thing I'd ever expect from you,' he drawled back and received a belligerent glare as Kate jerked to her feet.

She wasn't going to stick around while he made jokes at her expense. Furiously she began throwing clothes in her case and ignored him when he came to stand at her shoulder.

'Listen, Kate, I know my father's upset you. But let's not over-react, okay?' he suggested on a reasonable note that made Kate want to scream.

'Over-react!' She rounded on him, eyes bright with temper. 'I'm not over-reacting. It's you!'

'Me?' His brows drew together in genuine surprise. 'All things considered, I thought I was behaving quite calmly.'

'Exactly! Why can't you for once act like any normal person would?' she flared back and was subjected to a searching look before he caught on.

'I get it. You imagined I'd be mad when I read the report and I guess I might have been . . . well, if I didn't know you better by now,' he assured her but the quiet statement scarcely had the soothing affect intended.

'Oh, so you don't find the idea of my selling guns to a load of terrorist murderers in the least bit out of character?' Kate challenged, her voice strident with anger and hurt.

'Now hold on, Kate.' He raised his hands, an appeal for her to listen. 'You're jumping to the wrong conclusions. What I meant was, I don't believe——'

'I'm jumping to the wrong conclusions,' she cut in, even more inflamed. 'That's rich coming from you, Fitzgerald! First I was a—what was the word—a hooker, yes? Then I was living with a man. And what's the latest—a gold-digger, maybe?'

'Kate,' he gave her an indulgent look, 'what are you talking about?'

'Oh, come off it, I know what your father would have insinuated about a girl with my background. But you'd never think it, would you?' she quoted derisively and not giving him a chance to reply for himself, accused bitterly, 'Like hell you wouldn't! Was that the game, Van—play me along to see if I was after you for your money?'

'You tell me—you seem to know all the answers,' he

drawled, undisguised mockery that was the final straw for Kate.

Whirling round to slam shut her suitcase, she went to lift it off the bed, only to have the locks snap open and her clothes scatter everywhere—the dramatic gesture completely ruined.

And as if it were his fault, she turned again and nearly screamed in her frustration, 'You're no better than that devious, scheming, bigoted father of yours!'

Intended as the ultimate insult, it did indeed prove too much for Van. But if Kate expected anger, she was not at all prepared for the reaction she did get.

He was *laughing*! He was actually laughing. Struggling not to perhaps, but scarcely managing as he replied, 'I'm sorry, Kate, but really—you can't mean all that garbage.'

It was the word garbage that did it—snapped what little control Kate had left as her hand rose to slap the infuriating grin from his face.

Only his reflexes were quicker for his head jerked back and a hand caught hers on the downward curve; then before Kate could even think to use her other hand in this uneven contest, he had made to grab it too, taking her off-balance as he did.

Together they fell on to the clothes now strewn across the bed and lay there, eyes inches apart. Neither moved. Breath held, time suspended, they simply stared at one another—the laughter gone from his face, the fight from hers.

Then wondering how anger could die that quickly, and hate become love so intense it must be revealed in her every feature, Kate tried to look away.

'No, Kate—not this time,' he said on a groan and a hand gripped her chin, compelling acknowledgement of the desire flowing between them as his mouth slowly lowered towards hers.

Almost at the first touch of his lips, Kate's parted for him, a sweet moan of submission rising in her throat as her pride gave way. Endlessly they kissed, with a passion so stark they might have already been lovers, so deep Kate felt she must be pouring her heart out to him without saying a word. Yet when he lifted his head, there was a question in his eyes and he drew away from her until just a hand smoothed the tumbled hair from her face.

It was as though he was still uncertain of her, unaware of her feelings for him. Perhaps it should have made it easier to do the *right* thing. Somehow it didn't. Instead she saw in his eyes such longing for her, it was painfully like a promise of love. And in that moment, loving him was all that seemed to matter. Her arms reached out for him as she echoed huskily, 'No, Van, not this time,' before drawing his mouth back to hers.

He led her gently that first time they made love and later she came to realise every move he made, he made for her—and to recognise the restraint in the soft, unhurried caress of his hands gently pushing aside her clothing, the lips brushing against her skin, their touch a sensual, lingering torment.

He was a silent lover, but when she lay naked before him, pale and lovely in the gathering shadows of evening, his eyes expressed the pleasure he found in simply looking at her. They never left her as he stood by the bed, removing his own clothes. And their warm gaze wandering down her slender body, touching and dwelling with breathtaking intimacy, made her feel he was already making love to her in his mind. Yet that possessiveness aroused need not shame, and her only fear was the fear of disappointing.

Then he lay down beside her and at the first exquisite shock of his bare skin against hers, her thoughts scattered to leave pure instinct. Unerring instinct as she entwined her body with his, and sent a shudder of desire running through him. Sweet instinct as she slid her arms up his chest to clasp round his neck, and bring his searching mouth down on hers.

Together they turned, locked in each other's embrace, Kate sinking back against the bed and trembling when his lips trailed down her neck in a slow sensuous path to her breasts; Kate arching to him while his mouth pulled gently, then sucked hungrily on each swollen nipple; aching for him as his hand spread against her stomach where desire curled like a flame.

Higher and higher he led her so every move *she* made, was an unconscious invitation—sweeter and more alluring until all at once he lifted away from her. In startled protest her eyes flew open but dilated at the sight of him poised above her, his face naked with emotion as he savoured the moment he took what was now lovingly offered.

Roused beyond thought or fear, that first downward thrust of his body was like a betrayal in the pain it brought. At its initial shock, she might have pushed him off if he hadn't held her to him, let her punish him with the scratch and bite of her nails while he turned his head to murmur soothing, loving words in her ear. Surprisingly the tearing pain was quick to subside and, believing from his stillness their lovemaking over, she felt an empty ache in its place.

When she uncurled her fingers from his shoulders, he suddenly raised his head and to Kate's shame, caught the disappointment in her eyes. Too late she tried to blank it off. Bemused, she saw a knowing smile form on his lips. Naively unaware of what it meant, her eyes actually widened in astonishment when he began to move against her once more, and a soft laugh greeted her first gasp of wondering pleasure at the sensation before he too lost himself in the sweetness of her response. Hands spreading on his back, she seemed to urge him nearer, then gradually moved with him, rising to meet each wave of passion, and when its tide finally rushed over them, clinging to him in drowning, dying ecstasy.

For Kate that feeling was slow to recede. When Van eventually rolled on to his back, cradling her to him, she was only remotely conscious of the movement. Senses dazed, she was content to drift, reluctant to surface into reality.

Yet as awareness returned, there was no regret in her heart for what had happened. A hand was stroking her hair, the other curving her against him, and in a poignant way, this gentle aftermath to their lovemaking touched her deeper than the act itself, helped her pretend love wasn't all one-sided.

Then he tilted her face upwards and she saw from his how foolish any pretence was. Making love hadn't changed things, merely confused them. If anything, his grimly serious expression suggested any regrets were his.

'Kate, are you all right?' he asked at her own deepening frown. 'I tried hard not to hurt you but——'

'Yes—yes, I'm fine,' she choked out in embarrassment.

But eyes creased with doubts, he disconcerted her further by murmuring back, 'You'll see, Kate. Next time, it won't——'

'No!' Abruptly she halted the soft undermining promise in his voice, and clutching the silk bedcover to her breasts, sat up away from him.

A hand reached out to prevent her escaping altogether as he demanded hoarsely, 'For God's sake, Kate, what's wrong? Are you sorry now—is that it?'

She shook her head but she kept her back to him. 'No, I knew what I was doing. It's just—I can't have an affair with you, Van. I wouldn't be able to take it . . .'

Her tone was quiet and unaccusing so she was unprepared for his yanking her off balance and shifting to hold her down against the bed.

'Dear God, Kate!' he exclaimed, eyes incredulous, 'You can't believe that's all I want from you—a goddamn affair!'

'Wh—what else?' she stammered in surprise.

'What the hell do you think?' he rasped back. 'I want you to marry me, of course.'

But when his words did sink in, Kate could only stare back at him with a look that questioned his sanity. His voice was a harsh bark, his fingers were biting into her arms—and he wanted to *marry* her?

'Well, say something,' he prompted as her silence threatened to be interminable.

'W-why?' she eventually managed.

'*Why?*' he echoed on an explosive note.

'Yes, why?' Kate repeated, beginning to recover her spirit.

'Because when a man proposes,' he said, jaw clenching, 'it's customary to give him an answer—like yes or no or I'll think about it?'

His sarcasm both hurt and angered Kate.'Then no!' she snapped back, and winced as his fingers tightened brutally on her arms.

'Is that all you're going to say—*no*?' He challenged her bare reply with a bitter fury that frightened Kate. Bewildered, she stared up at the cruel twist on his lips, wondering where the tender, gentle lover had so quickly gone.

Then at her lack of response, he levered himself away from her, growling, 'Well, I'm damned if I'm going to make a fool of myself by begging!'

And before Kate fully realised his intention, he had gathered up his discarded clothing and slammed the connecting door behind him. At first she simply lay where he'd left her, unable to move, to even cry. And when she rose from the bed, it was still in that mercifully numb state. Each action—dressing, lifting her case back on the bed, picking up her scattered clothes—was done automatically.

She was packed when Van reappeared in the doorway. He had dressed too. She looked at him blankly, as if he was a stranger. He began to move towards her and she held his eyes but that emptiness in hers remained. He stood before her, pain etched in deep lines on his face.

'Oh, Kate, what have I done to you?' The low, agonised question broke through her numbness and quite clearly she heard him groan, 'I love you so very much I thought I could make you love me too.'

It was shock that had her stammering back, 'Y-you love me?'

He nodded gravely. 'Too much, perhaps—but you must know that.'

Kate felt she was dreaming. How could he love her?

'You can't love me,' she whispered, more to herself than him. 'It's impossible after . . . after everything.'

'Well, I admit you made it difficult at times.' A hand

reached out to touch her cheek. 'But never impossible. The only impossible part is to stop loving you. Believe me, I've tried.'

'I've tried, too,' Kate found herself admitting quietly, and admitted more with her vulnerable expression.

'You mean . . .?' His face moved from a pained frown to a wondering smile, and then back again.

She helped him by echoing softly, 'Very much . . . too much,' and was suddenly in his arms, lifted off her feet in a fiercely possessive embrace. So fierce she half laughed, half cried, 'Van—you're hurting me.'

He set her back down on the ground and gazed at her with a look so loving she almost did cry. 'Are you sure?'

'About loving you, yes,' she said, smile shy.

'And about marrying me?' He held his breath for her answer and had it in the way her eyes shifted uneasily from his.

'You must know your father's right, Van,' she murmured sadly. 'Having a wife with my past would inevitably damage your future.'

'My future?' For a moment he was completely puzzled, then he gave a laugh of sheer incredulity. 'You haven't been taking that old man seriously, have you, Kate?'

'I—why shouldn't I?' She scowled slightly at the exasperated question, reminding him, 'You did say you'd come to an understanding with him.'

'Yeah, but not that kind. I just made it clear I have no intention of leaving England—far less entering American politics,' Van revealed, the hard note in his voice dismissing the idea the Senator had any influence over him.

'Oh,' Kate mumbled, beginning to feel she had been a little foolish.

A hand cupped her chin, forcing her to look up at him. 'What you see, Kate, is what you'd get—a writer with no ambitions beyond his next book and a quiet life shared with a certain young English girl. So if you need an excuse, tell me I'm too old for you or I'm not the man you want to spend the rest of your life with, but don't use my father. Okay?'

'Okay,' she gulped, feeling more foolish.

'Or your own father for that matter,' he went on forcefully, 'because I don't give a damn about him either. This is between us. It comes down to whether you want to marry me or not, nothing else. Either yes or no, Kate?'

He was right, Kate realised—it came down to a simple question. Did she love him or didn't she?

'Yes,' she said succinctly but Van obviously hadn't expected such a simple answer.

He frowned. 'Yes what?'

'Yes, *please*?' Kate offered with a smile that spread into a grin that matched his.

Then before she knew what was happening he had grabbed her hand and she was being dragged after him.

'Van, what are you doing?' she gasped as they reached the top of the stairs.

He paused long enough to plant a swift, hard kiss on her mouth and laugh back, 'Making damn sure you can't change your mind, sweet Kate.'

They found everyone gathered in the sitting room. What Kate best remembered was the pride and happiness in Van's voice when he announced she had agreed to marry him. She made no objection when he added—as soon as possible. She knew she was never going to change her mind about this brash, arrogant, lovely man at her side.

A delighted Ellen kissed her cheek, and teased, 'A misunderstanding, mm?' The boys grinned and Johnny said to Van, 'I knew you could do it,' as though he'd just conquered Everest. But no one seemed surprised—not even the Senator.

And turning to catch Van's eyes on her, she began to think she had been very blind not to see the love in them before, and very cowardly in not putting a name to her own feelings long ago.

'Look,' he murmured under his breath and Kate followed his amused gaze to find the Senator raising his glass, then inclining his head to her. 'He's telling you

you've won. I only hope you like the prize.'

Kate smiled up at him with a trust in her eyes that told him how she felt about the *prize*.

A man worth knowing, a man worth loving.

Harlequin Presents

Coming Next Month

Available in April wherever paperback books are sold, or through Harlequin Reader Service:

In the U.S.
P.O. Box 1397
Buffalo, N.Y.
14240-1397

In Canada
P.O. Box 2800, Postal Station A
5170 Yonge Street
Willowdale, Ontario M2N 6J3

You're invited to accept 4 books and a surprise gift Free!

Acceptance Card

Mail to: **Harlequin Reader Service®**

In the U.S.	In Canada
901 Fuhrmann Blvd.	P.O. Box 2800, Postal Station A
P.O. Box 1394	5170 Yonge Street
Buffalo, N.Y. 14240-1394	Willowdale, Ontario M2N 6J3

YES! Please send me 4 free Harlequin Presents® novels and my free surprise gift. Then send me 8 brand new novels every month as they come off the presses. Bill me at the low price of $1.75 each ($1.95 in Canada)— an 11% saving off the retail price. There are no shipping, handling or other hidden costs. There is no minimum number of books I must purchase. I can always return a shipment and cancel at any time. Even if I never buy another book from Harlequin, the 4 free novels and the surprise gift are mine to keep forever.

108 BPP-BPGE

Name _____ (PLEASE PRINT)

Address _____ Apt. No. _____

City _____ State/Prov. _____ Zip/Postal Code _____

This offer is limited to one order per household and not valid to present subscribers. Price is subject to change.

ACP-SUB-1R

No one Can Resist . . .

HARLEQUIN REGENCY ROMANCES

Regency romances take you back to a time when men fought for their ladies' honor and passions—a time when heroines had to choose between love and duty . . . with love always the winner!

Enjoy these three authentic novels of love and romance set in one of the most colorful periods of England's history.

Lady Alicia's Secret by Rachel Cosgrove Payes

She had to keep her true identity hidden—at least until she was convinced of his love!

Deception So Agreeable by Mary Butler

She reacted with outrage to his false proposal of marriage, then nearly regretted her decision.

The Country Gentleman by Dinah Dean

She refused to believe the rumors about him— certainly until they could be confirmed or denied!

Everyone Loves . . .

HARLEQUIN GOTHIC ROMANCES

A young woman lured to an isolated estate far from help and civilization . . . a man, lonely, tortured by a centuries' old commitment . . . and a sinister force threatening them both and their newfound love . . . Read these three superb novels of romance and suspense . . . as timeless as love and as filled with the unexpected as tomorrow!

Return To Shadow Creek by Helen B. Hicks

She returned to the place of her birth—only to discover a sinister plot lurking in wait for her. . . .

Shadows Over Briarcliff by Marilyn Ross

Her visit vividly brought back the unhappy past—and with it an unknown evil presence. . . .

The Blue House by Dolores Holliday

She had no control over the evil forces that were driving her to the brink of madness. . . .